# OUTSIDE THE LINES

Ameera Patel

**CATALYST PRESS**
Pacifica, California

In North America, this book is distributed by
Consortium Book Sales & Distribution, a division of Ingram.
Phone: 612/746-2600
cbsdinfo@ingramcontent.com
www.cbsd.com

Originally published by Modjaji Books in South Africa.

FIRST EDITION
10 9 8 7 6 5 4 3 2 1

ISBN 978-1-946395-35-1

Library of Congress Control Number 2019953236

Printed in India by Imprint Press

# OUTSIDE THE LINES

Ameera Patel

# CATHLEEN

She is usually fine with being alone but tonight the unfamiliar faces make her feel cold. They stare out looking at no one in particular. A sea of mannequins jerking awkwardly to the offbeat of the music. She is unseen. She pretends she is the lead in her own music video, walking through a sea of extras paid not to look at her. She is golden—a god, extending from the retro carpet up to the dark ceiling. She grinds her teeth, straining against each other. The enamel squeaks in time with the DJ's trigger finger. She scans the room. Her eyes are a torch. Searching. But there is no soothing familiarity. No calm. No exciting leap of her stomach with the recognition of safety in a face across the room. She wades through the crowd. Its heaviness peels away at her skin as she forces her way toward the toilets.

The wooden door is swollen from damp and opens to hipster girls in the chipped mirror, reapplying eyeliner beneath their wide-rimmed glasses. Their eyes are judgmental and visionless. There's an open stall and she finds refuge with a turn of the silver lock. The toilet has no lid. She wipes a tiled ledge below the window with some toilet paper. Then she taps her little plastic bag and allows some of the white powder to fall out. Two fingers swipe the edge of the card and then rub across her gums. She pulls a ten rand note out of her purse. Roll up. Place on line. Block one nostril. Inhale, switch and repeat. It's funny, cocaine smells a lot like money—or maybe money smells like cocaine. She runs her fingers across the tile for any last traces of hope and finds a sense of calm. Okay.

She is as happy as Tammy who loves Brian so boldly she was willing to tell every user of this stall. How many other stalls has Tammy been into? Has this confession been witnessed across the city? What if things don't work out for the two of them? Will Tammy return to every stall and adjust the statement? "Tammy loves Brian—no more." Or will the lie remain printed across peeling walls until the cheap-arse owners finally decide to whitewash the young lovers away? There's a knock on the door. Her chipped nails flush the clean bowl and unlatch. She is ready.

The wide eyes of girls in line for the toilets stare as she lifts her chin and checks her nose for white crusties. She's clean, but continues to stare. She removes her hair band. It's knotted with blonde strands twisted into each other. She shakes her head but her hair is oily. The strands have matted together. Her fingers work at separating the clumps of hair. If only she could arrange them more interestingly, maybe people won't notice the dirt. She finally settles on a disheveled messy do, like the start of a bird's nest. Wiping a piece of tissue beneath her eyes, she removes the black sediment left by her eyeliner. She pops a piece of Infinity gum into her already-gyrating mouth and readies herself for the pulse vibrating through the wooden door. A careful application of blood red lipstick completes the look and she smiles at herself. Her mind races. The girls in line are all dressed the same. They're everything that's wrong with the world. Identical and scratching away at their individuality to become one pus-filled blob. She tries to hold onto the thought, but it slips away. The butter fingers of her mind are unable to catch it. She doesn't panic. Fresh topics of conversation will appear with the same ease that these have disappeared. She's ready. She's open.

The lighting has changed and the extras are on a break. Their eyes have been given permission to notice her but there is hesitation in their body language.

She is the unapproachable pseudo-celebrity in the room.

Patting her new hairdo, she struts to the bar and waves a hundred rand note at the bartender.

"What can I get you, honey?" His teeth have started to discolor; yellow-brown patches have begun to form.

"A shot of tequila and a double vodka with water." She takes the shot, turns and faces the room. She scans it once more. She's not looking for the familiar any longer. The room has broken into groups. The serious dancer types circle the DJ, praising his alternative mixes, sweat racing down their bodies and into their high-top sneakers. Groups of girls and guys play obvious mating games between the bar and the darker corners of the room. Smaller gatherings, in heated debates, decorate the tables. She spots another single. He walks to the bar. She was looking for more. She was looking to feel alive, for someone to make the night extraordinary. He is underwhelming. He sits down next to her.

"You on your own?" His eyes are fiery but his face is long and thin, like the face of a horse.

"No, I'm not. There are at least seventy people around."

He smiles, exposing little gaps between his teeth. A coin could get stuck in one of those gaps.

She laughs. "Yes, I'm alone."

He buys her a tequila.

The wonderful thing about coke is that it helps with feeling sober. She is lucid and loving her own company. Her overactive mind tries to focus on the freshness in his eyes. It's the only part of him that is anywhere close to being attractive. If she stares into his eyes for long enough, will the rest of him improve? She wants to like him, despite his badly tailored short-sleeved shirt and gold chain. He could make the night bearable, so she stares deep into his eyes trying hard to avoid the bland background of his face. He seems to be enjoying the attention. She's making him feel special but keeps blanking on his name.

"The only reason I keep forgetting it is because it doesn't suit your face," she explains. "You look like an Eddie." And that's what she calls him for the rest of the night.

"What kind of a party are you looking for tonight?" He squints at her.

"It depends, do you have any mix?" She plays his game but is not yet certain that she's ready to share her stash with him.

"I have a two liter in the car." He smiles his gap-toothed smile.

She assumes he means two grams and they head outside.

The air is a crisp wake up call. Little raised bumps appear on her skin. Eddie hustles into a tattered black jacket. He puts his arm around her and steers her down the street and around the corner to a small blue car. She doesn't know much about cars but she does know that this one is particularly dirty. It smells like old McDonald's and feet inside. She's forced to open a window. The cold air keeps her alert. He starts the car and drives to an isolated spot. It probably wasn't a good idea to leave with him. She should've waited inside while he went to fetch the coke. They could have done it in the toilets, like she usually does. But here they are. The two of them, parked in the middle of Joburg city at 1:30 in the morning. High-rise buildings loom like giants over them. She startles at every little sound. The streets in this part of town are dark and empty. She wants to tell him to turn the ignition back on and head back to the people but doesn't want to seem paranoid. Plus, he's already started to decant his sachet on the dashboard so they can't move until they've done it.

"You want to go first?" He hands her a note.

She takes a line. She starts to relax. They're safe here, she decides.

He takes a line and hands the note back to her. There are four more lines on the dashboard. They finish them quickly.

He offers her a cigarette. His soft pack is crumpled and the cigarette that comes out of it is bent. She taps it against the dashboard and puts it to her lips. He strikes a match, cupping his hand around the flame to protect it from non-existent wind. The back of her throat burns a little. Before she knows it, the cigarette is finished.

She lights another.

He runs his hand through her hair and starts to undo the extravagant nest. His hands rub hard against her scalp and she closes her eyes. Her hair feels thick and soft under his touch. His fingers are calloused, with uneven nails that snag her hair. They slip down to her neck. He pulls her head toward him and pokes his thin tongue into her mouth. All she can think of is a bird feeding its baby.

He looks at her. The twinkle is gone. "You have shit under your nose." He looks away as she flips the mirror on the sun visor down. She sees herself. She sees puffed-up semicircles under the eyes of a sunken face. She looks old.

He starts to cut more lines but she continues to stare. Her hair has separated into fine strands. She runs her fingers along the exposed scalp. He looks at her. She ties it up into a rat's tail resting on her spine. She looks sick, a resemblance of what her mother looked like during chemotherapy. The difference was that her mother had something to lose. Her mother was once a striking woman with thick glossy hair and there was never a need to try. No make-up or accessories were needed. She remembers being comforted by the strands that fell from her mother's head when she got sick—pleased that people could believe that this woman was her mother. Before the sickness, they had tried everything to get Cathleen's hair right: pills, oils, different shampoos including ones for balding men. It was embarrassing. She was almost glad when her mother found herself in the same position. She was happy that there was nothing to stop it from falling out and they could both be ugly together. What must it have been like for a woman, whose beauty spoke before she did, to have a child that no one could even call pretty? People would look at Cathleen and say, "Ag shame" and "What a well-behaved child." She used to hope that she would grow into her mother. Instead, her mother grew to look more like her.

"Your turn, sweetness." Eddie hands over the note.

"My name is Cathleen, not sweetness." She realizes the strangeness of the situation.

"That's pretty fucking rich coming from the girl who renamed me in the bar." His eyes have lit up, anticipating a fight.

"Cathleen means pure! My mother named me when she saw the blond halo around the head of the baby she birthed. That is significant Eddie. You, on the other hand, are named after a horse," she spits at him.

"That's enough for you then! Get the fuck out!" He snatches the note from her and leans over to open the passenger door. "Who do you think you are? You half-balding pig! The only reason I came to speak to you is because you were alone and grinding your jaw like you were already two grams down." He starts to push her out of the car.

"Please, I'm sorry, please." She can't get out, not here in this deserted place. This part of town is confusing. She'll never be able to get back. She holds onto the edge of the seat and pleads. "I'll do whatever you want, I'm really sorry. I didn't mean it. I'm just fucked. Please. I'll do anything." She grabs at his hand and shirt and almost spills some of the coke on the dashboard. He holds her hands firmly and allows her back in. She sits down and closes the door.

He starts to take a line. His nose is giving him difficulty. He swaps nostrils and finishes it. He hands her the note, but as she reaches for it, he pulls it away.

"You said you would do anything." His eyes are shifty but his voice is controlled. She waits for his demands.

"I want to see you." His hands move to unzip her jersey. He slips the fabric over her shoulders. He looks down and moves his hands to her thighs and fingers her woolen slip dress. It peels up over her hips and she lifts her arms to allow it to come off completely. A cold hand grapples with the bra strap. It is undone. He tells her to take off her panties, and with shaking hands, she obliges.

She doesn't look up but he places the note in her eye line. She takes it and snorts the coke, aware of his eyes on her.

"Face me." The calmness of his voice sends ripples of fear through her but she turns her head toward him.

"No." He taps her knee. "Your body...point yourself at me."

She turns, leaning her back against the coldness of the glass and shifts her legs to face him. He separates her legs. She's shaking but can't bring herself to do anything.

Her head is ringing.

Her body is wearing a large gray trench coat. It's dragging her down as she walks into a sparsely furnished flat.

Eddie hands her a glass of vodka.

He's got some more coke and is sitting on the only couch in the room, cutting lines on a clear table. She sits on the fake leather; it is cracked, white insides exposed.

They are talking. Muffled sounds crawl out of her mouth.

What is this conversation about? Words fly into the room. She tries to grab at them. If she could hold onto them, maybe she could piece them together? They won't stay still for long enough to make sense.

Her body is pounding and her breath is shallow. She asks for a cigarette. Finally, she manages to take something in. The burning inside her is a reassuring familiarity.

They take more lines.

She makes promises.

The conversation is too familiar and she hears her mother's name crash into this unknown space too many times.

She shivers under the coat.

He refills their glasses in the kitchen.

She takes another line.

He puts music on. It feels like it's pounding out from under her skin. She stands and sways along with it. Eddie comes to her and takes off the coat covering her. He throws it onto the couch and leans back to watch her. She runs her hands down her body. Where are her clothes?

Sunlight strokes her head into a state of nausea. She tries to cover her head but a body is weighing her down. Her breathing is shallow under the mass pressing down on her lungs. She is trapped. The room is small and encroaching. It takes all the strength left in her depleted body and one exhausting push to get him off.

She's alone in the room. Her throat is dry.

A man stands in the doorway. His face is blurred. He is in a suit and has a red skinny tie. He smiles at her and leaves.

# 2

# FLORA
*Small with long thin fingers that are always reaching*

She's organizing the papers on the dining room table but can't stop looking at the clock. It's an old clock, with wiry silver arms. The second hand doesn't seem to be moving. He's never late. It is two minutes to eight. He's been clouding her mind since she woke up. The lines across his forehead, the soft shy glances of his eyes and his body. His is a dependable body that rises and falls with the precision of time. It started when they first met. She didn't know that men like that existed anymore. His friend was a real chatterbox, going on and on about nothing. But the painter silently took her in. No one has ever looked at her in such a way. What was it that he saw? She felt like there was space to show him everything. It was terrifying the first time, but she's getting used to those looks.

Why won't he come already?

She gathers up the empty beer bottles in the lounge and walks to the bin. There's only one bin now, a single silver tube. The madam used to insist on recycling. It was complicated having to decide on which bin to use. Now all the rubbish is together. Flora washes her hands and dries them on a dishcloth before straightening out her dress. It's red like a plum. She doesn't want it to get messy before the painter sees it. A game of *Snake 2* will help the time go faster. She stands at the table, holding her phone.

This has to be the best time of day. The house is hers to do whatever she wants in it. She can work at her own pace without anyone getting in her way. The early mornings are too hectic. Seven-year-old James can never leave without forgetting one thing or the other. He is always searching through things and asking her to find a book or a bag or a cricket bat. He must start packing his things the night before. But Mr. Joseph is worse, bumbling around like a half-drunk bear with a sore head; it makes her flustered. She finds herself having to swerve around him in the mornings. He can't help get his own son ready for school, always lost in his own head, walking back and forth mumbling to himself.

The bell rings.

She leaps into the air. The painter has arrived and she can't contain her excitement. She drops her phone on the table and rushes to the cupboard with the cleaning supplies, almost tripping over one of James's games. She grabs the Windolene, a dry cloth and an old newspaper. They are the perfect tools to disguise her fascination. She strategically positions herself in front of the window closest to where he will start painting.

The bell rings again.

She rushes to the intercom and lets him in at the gate. Beads of sweat have gathered just below the start of her hairline from all the excitement. She wipes them away and starts to work. She wants to look like she has been busy all along.

He walks past the window and straight to his paint supplies. His shoulders lead his body as he moves. He bends down and starts to open the paint tin. There is something tender about the way he is with the paint. He slides the back end of a paintbrush into the groove between the lid and the tin, encouraging the tin to open rather than forcing it. He presses down slowly until the lid pops off.

He glances up and waves at her.

Her insides jive.

She sprays the window and wipes away the moisture to reveal him in clarity. She used to hate washing windows. These windows have never been cleaner. He dips his brush into the paint and starts to work. His face softens as his arm strains up and down. He moves smoothly, almost like a cat. She can imagine him becoming ferocious if it were ever necessary. His body is powerful. He looks at her again and she thinks she sees him smile. The softness of his lips has her grinning back. She can't stop herself and sprays the window. He must think that she is absolutely ridiculous. She gives the window one last wipe and goes to the kitchen.

Flora is not used to feeling shy. The last time a man made her feel like this was at least twenty years ago and ended up being a huge mistake. She is too old to make that mistake again. She is always warning Zilindile about passion. A fire can be warm but it dirties the air and eventually everyone is left coughing. Lust blurs reason. Relationships must be based on logic otherwise there's no security. She won't be acting on her impulses any time soon. If you don't stoke the fire, it will die on its own.

But there's nothing wrong with washing windows.

Water and Sunlight liquid fill the sink. She swirls her hand in the water, encouraging more bubbles to form. Dipping the dishes into the water, she thinks of washing him. What would his skin feel like? She's felt his hands but his chest must be better, probably warm and hard. She would caress the different hues of brown on his body and would take care not to rub too hard on the sunburnt areas.

She wipes her hands. These are not the thoughts of any good Christian woman. She is going to need to pray extra hard, if this keeps up.

She sits down at the table and starts a game of *Snake 2* on her phone. She moves her thumb expertly. The snake grows rapidly. The painter is at the front door. Her snake runs straight into a wall. He has a bunch of flowers clutched so tightly the stems must be bruised. Maybe he is also a Christian? Mr. Joseph planted the flowers along the edge of the house. If Mr. Joseph were still gardening, there would be hell to pay. She holds her hand out to receive them. "Thanks. Ready for your tea?" Her voice shifts into a higher register when she speaks to him. He nods. It's a simple nod but to her, it's more. A specific nod. Not rushed. It's a thought out decision to agree. A definitive yes.

She switches the kettle on and takes yesterday's flowers out of the vase and puts them on the table. As she fills the vase with fresh water, she can feel his eyes on her. It's not an intrusive stare but it's making her warm, like his eyes are smiling at her actions. She has never been given flowers with such regularity. The first time he brought her flowers, she was annoyed. She thought that he was trying to say something about the way she decorated the house but it has become a welcomed routine.

The kettle groans and exhales hot air into the kitchen.

# CATHLEEN
*Handfuls at a time*

The bedding is heavy. It feels like the duvet is filled with weights. She kicks it off the bed and rolls to the other side where the sheet is still crisp.

It's too cold.

She crawls back across the bed and leans over to get the duvet. She only manages to get half of it back onto the bed and tightly rolls herself beneath it. Her eyes are burning but they won't stay closed. Her jaw on the other hand is clenched tight. She needs a release. If she could get some weed, she might be able to calm herself and fall asleep.

She crouches on the floor, scouring through the contents of her bag. Beneath an empty cigarette box and random slips, is her wallet. It's empty. How could she have spent all her money? She can't even remember opening her bag. How did she get home? It's all fucked. Her face is hot and her mind is racing. There are too many blanks in her memory to place anything. Who was she with? She remembers dropping a glass and moving away from the broken pieces because she was barefoot. When did she take her shoes off?

She goes to her bookshelf and pulls out all the books and stupid ornaments. She still has a ridiculous green-haired troll doll. She used to love those things. More books and magazines are displaced onto the floor. She used to hide loose cigarettes all over her room. Now that she needs one, there's nothing. On the middle shelf, she sees her jewelry boxes. Her mother would bring her a new box every time she went away for work. She checks inside them. Some are filled with jewelry and others contain her school stationery. Cathleen loved having a different-looking pencil case from the other girls at school.

There's a five rand coin at the bottom of a silver box decorated with ruby elephants. It's enough to get two loose smokes. She rubs her hands together. Her palms are itching as if ants were crawling beneath her skin. One more gram and she will be able to think clearly again.

Her father's not home yet. He was such a bastard about giving her money last night, asking her all these questions. She didn't know where she was going or who she would see there. What difference would it make to him in any case?

He wouldn't give her any more today even if he was home. He's been really difficult to deal with lately. It's like he can't get his mind straight; one minute he's caring and interested and the next it's like he doesn't even see her.

She could sell something. She sits down amongst the pile of books, stationery and jewelry to see if there's anything expensive. Only her costume jewelry is left. She's already pawned off all the real stuff. It would take too long to go to the pawnshop, and she doesn't feel like leaving the house right now.

She needs cash.

She chews on the edges of her ridged stubby nails, taking off lines of nail polish with her teeth.

James might have money. Her dad always gives James whatever he asks for. Where's her phone? What's the time? James will still be at school. He might have something in his room. She goes to check through the pockets of his jeans. James's room is almost as messy as hers. She peels through the clothes lying on the floor. She can smell her armpits but it feels like the smell is being excreted from every pore of her body. There's a ten rand note in one of his jacket pockets. It's not enough. She tosses the jacket onto the heap of clothes. She owes too many people money. James's cupboard is still relatively neat. It's easy to finger through the hanging clothes. She finds a cigarette. The tip is squashed, but for a moment she feels triumphant. Why does James have a cigarette? Does he smoke? He's still a kid. She will have to talk to her dad about this. She lights up. It's beautiful.

She heads to her father's room. There are two twenty rand notes on his bedside table. If she takes one, he will probably notice. But if both are gone, he will just think he misplaced the money.

She grabs them and almost knocks a picture frame over. It's a black and white photograph of her mother. There's something mischievous about the way that her mother looks—her head slightly cocked to one side and the slightest smile, like she just told the photographer a secret.

Her father's clothes produce another fifty.

It's not enough but it's something. Zee will be able to help. He always manages to get her something. She goes back to her room and sends him a text.

Zee will bring some coke over in a few minutes. He has leftovers from last night. She puts the cigarette out on her windowsill and tosses the butt into the garden. She texts him again and asks him to bring cigarettes. She sits down and grabs one of the books on the floor to pass the time. The lines are jumpy. She can't focus. The words blend into each other. She could watch TV but Flora is downstairs. Being preached to right now is not what she's in the mood for.

This is her house. What makes Flora think she can get away with such attitude? Living with Flora is worse than having the pope as a grandfather. She pulls the duvet onto her. Flora is a righteous bitch. If Flora knew what her precious son was doing, it would knock her right off her high horse.

Flora used to be chilled. She was the one that Cathleen and James would run to whenever their mother shouted at them. She used to be easy to talk to. Flora was the first person to know if Cathleen failed a test or liked a boy or if anything interesting happened at all. Flora would be very hurt if Cathleen told her about Zee. There have been many moments when Cathleen wanted to expose it all, have it all out in the open, especially when Flora was in one of her mother superior moods. But that would make things difficult for Zee. He doesn't deserve that and Cathleen needs him.

The room is too hot.

She opens a window but the air outside is freezing. She pulls on a jersey and sees Zee walking toward the house. Finally! Maybe he'll stay and hang out with her. If he gets high, it'll be easier to get him to go and get more later.

# 4

# RUNYARARO
*Four teeth force their way out of the off-white smile. where space is a luxury*

His hand flicks upward at the wrist with the start of each new stroke. He breathes in time with the movement of the brush, inhaling as his hand slides up and exhaling as it comes back down.

This movement is not new to him. It sits deep within his body's memory and frees his mind, allowing him to find a sense of calm usually associated with meditation. The brush and his hand have become one, blending like the creamy-colored paint that coats the wall. The strokes are long and solid. They allow him to believe that beauty is simple.

If only the broken cracks of the world could be covered by Dulux. He would use the whole range from Lemon Meringue to Midnight Blue. Craters would fill with velvet thickness. He has seen what his work does for people by watching his past customers, as their homes were transformed before their eyes. Color speaks of character; color is imperative. Mr. Joseph's choice of beige was automatic, without any thought or discussion.

As he works, Runyararo can see it was a rash choice. It's a band-aid attempting to cover a cracked heart cavity. Warmth is missing. Perhaps a touch of daffodil yellow would help. Yes, if this was Runyararo's house it would be like a massive flower protruding from the cracked cement, claiming its space.

He has often thought of his dream home while fixing other people's houses. His house would be magnificent. It would call to people as they walked past, saying "Hello. How are you today?" and "Please come in for a cup of tea." It would be a polite house with no need for a mat to say welcome; the building itself would announce it to passersby. People would find it impossible to walk past without feeling the need to knock at the door, just to be given the chance to see what is behind the alluring exterior. Spellbinding, his house would speak the words he has always wanted to. A chatty place, well versed in small talk and full of jokes. On entering, no one would want to leave the humor and comfort. It would be the complete opposite of this silent spread-out house.

Is this the way that people experience his silence? Do they think of him as a vast empty vessel? Does he make them uncomfortable? Back home in Mutare, he longed for more space. It was claustrophobic. There were too many bodies and too many voices. The small space was drowned by the excessive noise. But this isn't any better. Here, the Josephs live past each other. There is more distance than he had from his neighbors in Mutare.

There, his neighbors were more like an extension of his family, except that Runyararo's family loved gossiping about them. "Did you see what she was wearing? We know she doesn't have anywhere to go." And, "He is getting so fat, if he was a girl the baby wouldn't be far from arriving." He was certain that he was often the subject of discussion in the house next door.

The Josephs look like they don't even know their neighbors' names, let alone enough information to gossip. What would they do if something happened?

He never thought that he would miss his annoying neighbors. He couldn't get them out of his business. There was no politeness in their timing. The toilet was the only place where he could find sanctuary, but he had a maximum of fifteen minutes in there until someone was banging on the door. Being at the Josephs' house is like being stuck in that toilet, undisturbed forever.

He hadn't wanted to leave Zimbabwe. Mutare was all he knew.

His mother's friend had a son called Shuvai. Shuvai was ten years younger than Runyararo but providing so much more money for his family, sending parcels from Johannesburg every month. Johannesburg terrified Runyararo. It was a foreign entity he never thought he would understand.

But as soon as he arrived, Shuvai began helping him. Shuvai is as good as a compass. Runyararo doesn't have any brothers but Shuvai is a natural fit. Shuvai talks so much that he doesn't seem to notice Runyararo's silence. Shuvai finds him work and he gives Shuvai money for his share of rent, food, transport and a little extra as a form of commission. What he has left is split equally between savings and money to send home. They stay together in a matchbox in Hillbrow. Hillbrow is dense, far more so than Mutare, and Runyararo misses his own clutter. He misses the noises he knew, the high-pitched chatter of his mother and sisters that filled the house. Now neighbors shout in foreign languages, and often unfamiliar noises wake him at odd hours of the night. He is torn between the stifled stillness of the Josephs' home and the mangled combinations of lifestyles in Hillbrow.

At least at the Josephs' he is left alone with the sweep of his brush against the wall. It is only when the family is home that the silence is unbearable. It seems to be getting worse by the day.

When he first arrived at the house in Parkview, they came across with the type of coolness that he had become accustomed to with white people. It is a cautious silence that doesn't question his quietness. By the end of the first week, he realized that this house is different from the others he's worked at. A droning hum tenses out from the walls and seems to push the family away from the boundary lines. They are always on the move, hardly ever uttering a word to each other as though the effort to speak above the heaviness in the air is too much. When they do speak, they shout. There is no middle ground.

How does Flora deal with them? An outsider living on the inside, she is attached to a family acting like acquaintances. By the end of the day he can at least leave, but she's there from before he arrives and is still there long after he leaves. What is it like when they are all at home? Her room is only three meters from the back door.

He can't stop himself from imagining the inside of her room. The possibilities of all it might contain are gloriously vast. She is one of the most stylishly dressed women he has ever seen. There is a brown skirt that hugs at her thighs, holding her legs together. It makes him desperate to peel her legs apart and blow some cool air between them. Her clothing is completely impractical for her work. He has seen her struggle when walking with heavy loads of washing or scrubbing the floor. But he likes that she takes care of herself. Perhaps her room is similarly unworkable, with luxurious furniture filling the smallness of the space. She appears to know that she is better than this.

She brings water, tea and lunch to him every day. Those moments are the ones he waits for. He gets to examine her more closely. Her slim fingers that wrap around his enamel mug are long and delicate. They look refined. But his favorites are her cheeky ankles, always peering at him from the bottom of her skirt. Those naughty ankles often show up in his dreams—the curve of the bone lined by a single pulsing vein that disappears up underneath her skirt.

How can the Josephs not notice her? She is bringing the washing outside. Water seeps onto her shirt from the basket, making the shirt cling to her chest. If only she would walk over to him. His fingers would look large undoing the buttons on her shirt. She looks at him briefly as she pegs the last item on the sagging washing line. He sees her smile but can't bring himself to wave. He looks back at the wall and notices that he has been repainting the same section since she came outside.

Mr. Joseph's daughter arrives home. She looks like a walking pile of pollution, contaminated with smells that a shower might not be forceful enough to remove. She ignores him and walks to the door at the same time as Flora. They don't greet each other. He's seen this behavior many times since he started working here. Flora walks slower than the girl but she has less distance to cover. They arrive at the door at the same time. The girl bumps Flora out of the way and enters without an apology. That grime shoving against Flora's elegant skirt is too much for him. He takes a step toward them. Flora turns back and looks at him. He wants to say something but moves back to the wall. Paint is easier than people. "Ag, children of today," Flora attempts to make it seem like nothing happened. She is telling lies, the way his mother did after the fights with his father. A bruised face and unsteady feet showed up the lie. It was never fine. But every time anyone asked, she lied more. He stopped wanting to ask. Stopped wanting to say anything at all. There were already too many lies in the world. He didn't need to add to them.

Now that familiar need to speak is back. He won't lie and agree with Flora. He is no longer that little boy, staring up at his mother's wounds. He is a man and Flora is a different body. A body he wants to protect and love. But his body stays facing the wall, neither nodding nor shaking his head. He gives Flora nothing, treating her in the same way that the Joseph family does. The thought of words, crawling their way out of his mouth, makes him feel ill, but saying nothing at all is sickness spreading. He stands there for the longest time, until he hears the door close, then he places his brush down on the tray and takes a seat in the garden.

He can't remember ever having words come out of his mouth. His mother used to say that he would tell her all his secrets but there are no pictures of those times in his mind. Silence sits far back in his memory, a blanket hushing previous voices. School was one of the hardest obstacles. A time filled with clenched fists, spitting mouths and disapproving teachers. He passed because teachers didn't want him in their class. Initially, there were accusations of insolence and pretending but after a while it was accepted. He was the regular annoyance, tossed from one class to the next. His not speaking became normal after a few years. Everyone got used to it. He was the child who was never spoken to because he didn't have a reply. Except for his mother and sisters, he was as unseen as he was unheard. Flora sees him but he has done nothing to help her. His silence is as harmful as words.

He goes back to work.

After two hours, the brush becomes heavy in his hand. He places it in the tray before examining his work. Half of the house is finished in beige, the other half still green; the past and the present are equal. He circles his hand around his wrist, loosening some of the tension, as he heads toward the house for a tea break. He passes the flowers, over-crowded bushes of color mixed with weeds. They're not good enough to make up for what he did, or rather didn't do. He doesn't want to interact with Flora right now.

Walking along the side of the house, he can feel how big it is; twenty people or more could live here with ease. He stays close to the paving along the side of the house, keeping off the overgrown grass, and wonders if Mr. Joseph will ask him to fix up the garden once the painting is done. He needs time to make it up to Flora. If he could re-design the garden, he would create a walkway leading to Flora's room. It would be lined by the most exquisite flowers he could find. The back door has been spoiled by rain making it difficult to pull open. His hand on the rusted handle is ready for the scrape of the wood against the floor.

Flora turns to look at him when he enters; she should be used to the groaning door by now. "You ready for some tea?" She doesn't seem upset by his empty hands. She doesn't seem to notice at all. He was being foolish. She probably thought it was a nuisance, having to re-place the flowers so regularly.

He waits in the doorway. She has been doing some ironing and places a perfect pile of white shirts on the dinner table before going to the kitchen. The table is made from a sturdy dark wood and is sur-rounded by twelve high-backed chairs. He can't imagine that many people here. Eating, laughter and happiness are out of place in this broken space. Besides being a resting area for clothes and the few papers strewn about, this table is an ornament, like a beaded giraffe bought on the side of the road. Its sole purpose is to decorate. The entire room has an unlived in feeling, like it's only there for show.

Flora brings him his tea and a few slices of buttered bread. He can't bring himself to look up at her. Keeping his eyes low, he takes his food to a shaded area in the garden, which he has turned into his eating space. He rests the cup and plate on a short tower of old bricks before pulling his seat, a large chunk of wood, closer to enjoy his meal. The tea is too sweet for his liking. He dips pieces of bread into it in order to even out the taste. The butter melts as soon as the bread touches the tea and an oily layer forms in the cup.

Shuvai loves having his tea this way; he can never have enough sugar in his cup. Shuvai organized this job for Runyararo and came with him, as he has done with Runyararo's other jobs in Johannesburg, to explain to the owner that Runyararo is a good worker but that he is mute. Then, because Shuvai likes girls too much, he likes to find the domestic worker to see if she's pretty and uses the way that Runyararo likes his tea as his reason for speaking to them. Flora is not Shuvai's type. Not only is she older, possibly a little bit older than Runyararo, but she is also a thin, small woman. Shuvai prefers the rounder ones, in fact the bigger the better.

But Shuvai is greedy for women like he's greedy for sugar so he tried to flirt with Flora. Runyararo thinks that Shuvai just wants to see how many women will fall for his one and only line: "If I had a woman like you, I wouldn't need any sugar because you are so sweet." He is very silly and still young, but he does get a lot of sugar. Flora was too ahead of her game to get caught up in Shuvai's nonsense and gave him a good telling off. Shuvai was so shocked by Flora's reaction his chin almost hit the floor. It was that attitude that first made Runyararo like her. Runyararo likes women who are fiery, but there haven't been many sparks since.

The gate scrapes against the cement driveway announcing Mr. Joseph's arrival before the soft hum of the white Volvo enters the yard. Runyararo slurps down the last of his buttery sweet tea and hurries toward the house. He leaves the cup and plate on the kitchen table and heads back to work. He pours fresh paint onto the tray. His brush is ready in his hand. He breathes deeply and relaxes into motion.

He is on his second stroke when Mr. Joseph trundles toward him. Mr. Joseph mutters something about time and hurrying up. The words are sprays of detergent poisoning the air, making it hard for Runyararo to breathe. A moment passes. Mr. Joseph's gaze remains firmly on the wall as though he is waiting for a response. Eventually, the heavy man sighs and walks along the path to the house. Runyararo places his paintbrush back into its tray and rests his hands on his knees to recover from the polluted air. He remembers the difficulties that words bring. A few minutes pass before he pulls himself together and sinks back into the paint and the walls. It's only four o'clock and he's certain that he can finish another large section within the hour. The sooner he finishes at this house, the better.

Inside the house, a swell begins. Mr. Joseph walks past the window that Runyararo is closest to, his mouth is moving and his head is shaking. Runyararo can't hear what Mr. Joseph is saying but a wave of unease moves toward the window and creeps through the panes to settle around him. Mr. Joseph moves into the next room and the wave retreats. Then he returns past the window, getting more frantic, his head moving every which way and his mouth opening and closing like a crazed cartoon. For his size, Mr. Joseph moves with an astonishing amount of speed. He picks up vases and bottles, moves picture frames around and then storms off again.

Runyararo tries to focus on the paint but it is no longer meditative, he cannot keep his eyes on the wall, they are too curious about what is happening inside. He has never seen the portly man behave like this. It is somehow exciting and terrifying, the way that Mr. Joseph moves in short sharp angles, like a truck attempting a three point turn in an overcrowded parking lot. Mr. Joseph picks up speed and the movement starts to look circular and almost drunken.

"Flaw-raaaaaaah!"

Why do white people call their workers with their voices rising like that? Do they think that black people only respond when their names are sung out in a strange chant?

Flora enters the room calmly; she's used to being summoned in that way, whether it's an emergency or simply to make a cup of tea. But she quickly sees Mr. Joseph's upset. Runyararo strains to hear exactly what is being said. Mr. Joseph is now talking softly with his mouth so tense that it is impossible to read his lips. He points at a vase with his thick doughy fingers. She goes to look inside it and then starts a strange circling dance of her own. Her hands fly into her hair and she shakes her head. Now they are both cartoons with quick moving mouths and large body movements. Runyararo is completely caught up and has to remind himself not to stand agape for all to see.

"Cathleen!" Mr. Joseph's voice is loud but doesn't do any tricks when he calls his daughter. She enters the room and the craziness continues. Flora is still circling. Mr. Joseph points at the vase again. The girl's behavior is strangely robotic. Her body is completely still but her eyes move from left to right. They stop suddenly as she looks at the window. Her rigid arm lifts and her finger aims at the point between Runyararo's eyes. Flora and Mr. Joseph turn sharply and stare at the man watching them through the window.

Runyararo can't look away and forces himself to place the paintbrush down when Mr. Joseph motions for him to come inside. The weight of his head falls through his body and sinks into his feet. It takes considerable concentration to move. One leaden foot follows the other. He thinks about bending each knee and raising each thigh in order to move toward the swollen door. He looks at the handle. He has never noticed that there are specks of green mixed with the rusting silver. His paint-stained fingers wrap around it and pull. He leans in to nudge the door open. There shouldn't be anything to be scared of but he wants to turn and run. As he closes the door behind him, he suddenly feels trapped. He wants to go back to his paint. He wants to blend. As he gets closer to the room, the image of that finger starts to poke into his chest. Flora has left the room and he is alone with the Josephs.

All of a sudden the house is too small. It is both cumbersome and empty. His hands refuse to be still. They rattle against the sides of his pants and tap out a random beat. The Josephs are standing with their backs against a large mirror. A crack runs across the left side of the mirror. A fearful version of Runyararo is split by the crack and reflects back at him. His challengers are ready for battle, their feet firmly planted and hands clenched. The man in the mirror, shaking and weak, is not a worthy opponent for them.

"We know what you did."

He stares at them as the bullets start to fly.

"You took the money from the vase." The girl points at him with her words; they both do.

He shakes his head and stands there, like a vowel without the shelter of consonants, as their words hit at him. They're on fire and he's disappearing in the smoke. He didn't think they had the power to suffocate him. He shakes his head, trying as hard as he can to disprove their claims and force sense back into his being.

"You didn't know stealing was wrong? You really are some kind of retard."

People are contaminated by their color. Runyararo remembers that certain things don't change. Color tells all and their color is beige; at least that's what they chose for themselves. He sees the red anger underneath their dull tone causing pink patches to creep through onto their faces and necks.

They see him and they see a thief, because he is new to them.

He is different.

"Just give us the money back, you fucking ..." It's easier for them to curse him, to make him the one who stole the money. He can see that it's just another lie. There are too many lies flying through the room. Their eyes blink incessantly and Runyararo can see that they don't believe their words either. They don't have any proof. All they have is words and poison. He is silent.

"Get out! Get out of here and don't come back unless you bring the money. You're lucky we haven't called the police. Our blacks don't have any problems with disciplining you foreigners."

This girl is too young to carry such hate. He leaves.

The roads have started to become busy. Cars speed through the suburb, trying to avoid the start of traffic. The city screams. His breathing is shallow but deepens as he walks. His belly rises. His body moves automatically, buildings pass by, large houses are replaced by busy roads until he looks up to see the familiar cracks of his Hillbrow home. Only eight floors until he can get some comfort. Eight floors of faces he barely recognizes. He didn't feel the journey. He can't feel his body. He doesn't feel anything at all. He sees the black gate, his black gate that opens with ease as his key turns. The door opens to welcome silence. It's a relief that Shuvai is not home.

He switches the kettle on, rinses out his mug and grabs a new teabag. They usually reuse teabags and he sees the one from this morning waiting for its second dipping, but now only a fresh bag will do. One teaspoon of sugar and he adds the hot water. He leaves the bag in the cup to soak until he's sure it's all used up. The tea is strong and allows him a moment to close his eyes.

## 5

# FRANK
## *A bear with no balance*

He hasn't done anything like that in years. Firing someone is awkward. It's both powerful and frightening. He was scared more than anything else. All the shouting came from fear.

Perhaps it was that Cathleen was standing there right next to him. She seemed to enjoy the power. She was so in control of her words, certain of what to say and how to say it. He hadn't planned on firing the guy but it all happened so fast, there was no way to stop it.

The painter didn't say anything. He just stood there, lost.

There was nothing intimidating about him. At one point, Frank wanted to stop it, the painter looked close to tears. But he had to stand firm next to his daughter. There was a strange thrill to it, like torturing insects when they were children. When they were small, Cathleen and Zilindile would steal his sunglasses case and fill it with as many ants as they could find. They would leave it on the kitchen table for him to find, by which time most of the ants had made their way out, much to Flora's dismay. Flora made up a range of horror stories about bugs to try and get them to stop. But that only served to boost Cathleen's enjoyment, and telling about Flora's reaction to the ants spreading across the table seemed to be just as much fun for Cathleen as filling the case.

She was always a mischievous child. She would climb into his lap at the end of the day and give her father a detailed explanation of all the tricks she had played. Frank never disciplined her for any of the tricks; he couldn't stop laughing at her gutsy behavior. Firing the painter was the first thing they had done together in ages. He should have stepped in and sent her to her room while he dealt with the painter. He is the parent. But he was lost in the moment.

He walks into the lounge. There is some cricket match on at Newlands. He sinks into the couch. It's getting old and makes groaning noises as he struggles to get comfortable. He reaches for the remote and feels the springs weakening under the worn material. The TV is showing a rerun of *Dr. Phil*. He can't find the DSTV remote.

What is he going to do about this house? He can barely afford the rates and taxes anymore, let alone the bond repayments. Jennifer's parents helped them buy the place. The payments were manageable with two salaries. It's too big for him to take care of alone. Too many things need replacing and he can't keep up.

Jennifer was good at sorting things out. She planned everything. If she were still around, they would be up early on Saturday morning and driving to a furniture shop, where she already knew which lounge suite she wanted. It would be delivered and fit in perfectly with the rest of the décor.

He lifts up the cushions and feels around the couch. He navigates his hand through a hole in the upholstery. Furry dust coats his fingers until he feels the cool plastic and brings the remote to the surface. Channel 202...but Dr. Phil continues to speak to some crying fat American.

He runs his hand through his graying hair. There are no batteries in the remote. He sighs. Just his remote control batteries, that's all he asks for. But these kids won't listen to him.

The couch groans as though it's relieved when he stands up.

He works through the channels on the decoder manually until the commentator's voice enters the room...*ever seen in SA cricket. We'll resume after tea.*

A commercial with naked talking babies takes over from the statistics. He's sure these babies are supposed to be endearing, but the voice-overs sound like they've been done by thirty-year-olds pretending they have never smoked.

Cathleen started smoking a few years ago. It smelled like she was using whole cans of deodorant to disguise it. He wanted to believe that she didn't. She told him smoker lies—they were in a bar or at a braai, and the cigarettes in her bag belonged to her friend Mary and Cathleen was only keeping them because Mary's parents would kill her if they found them. From his years as a teacher, he knew how to spot the lies. He could take one look at a teenager and know exactly what kind of trouble he was in for. But he didn't ask Cathleen what she thought he would do if he found the cigarettes.

It was easier with his students. There were measures in place: detention, the principal's office and the threat of phoning in parents kept his boys in line. But he always wanted to believe his daughter.

When she was born, she was so small in his arms, so fragile. From that minute he should have known that he was never going to be good at disciplining her. He fell in love so hard and fast, he stopped breathing as she curled into his arms.

Maybe she knew there weren't going to be any consequences.

She was eventually throwing cigarette butts all over the garden. She blamed the painter for that. Frank was too tired to argue. He wished the painter was smoking instead of stealing. Now he has to find a replacement before the house goes on show.

He still hasn't told the kids. But he's sure they could all do with a new start. They need to leave this house and get out of Johannesburg. Parkview is a contained environment. It was the perfect place to raise a family. But now all the shops, all the roads, the big trees and this house, they all feel like Jennifer. She loved Johannesburg. He needs somewhere new, where they can all start again. The children are slipping through the cracks. He can't get Cathleen to spend one night at home. After Jennifer died, he let Cathleen do whatever she wanted. He didn't have the strength to stop her. Jennifer's clothes are still hanging in the cupboard, waiting for her to return. Living here is like living in a hiatus. A new place will mean new rules. The children need him to guide them. Cape Town can be that start.

The painter's face keeps coming back to him. Eyes wide and mouth tightly shut. Cathleen wouldn't lie about such a thing, would she? He hardly knows her anymore, but he needs to believe her. The guy didn't defend himself.

Perhaps he could finish the painting himself. That way he could save some cash. Maybe he could rope Cathleen in as well—and James, and they would all have a chance to bond with each other. When she was little, Cathleen used to trail after him, wanting to help fixing odds and ends.

The three of them painting together, it would be the perfect time to tell them about selling the house. Knowing Cathleen, she would probably demand to be paid more per hour than that painter.

What was the painter's name again? His friend said it on the first day. One of those long and complicated ones that don't stick in his head. In all his years of teaching, the thing he was most proud of was being good with names. The boys appreciated it. These days his mind can't hold onto anything.

It's probably a good thing that he fired the painter. The painter was alone with Flora every day. He could have cleaned them out. What would Frank have said to the police? That a tough-looking foreign black man, who can't talk, but who he's pretty sure lives somewhere in Hillbrow, did it. They would laugh him right out of the station.

That's it. No more strangers on the property.

The painter had an almost architecturally perfect muscular build.

His forearms and biceps were chiseled into immaculate shape. If they had got into a fight, there would have been no competition.

There was a time when he used to be fit. He loved going to the gym. It's not easy to be sixty and have a flat stomach. The other day the painter lifted his shirt to wipe his forehead and revealed the kind of abs that appear on the cover of *Men's Health* magazine. Frank had fought hard to keep his belly in check. The painter ate a loaf of white bread, spread thick with butter, every day. Jennifer and he had been into all sorts of health fads. They tried high-fiber, low-GI, Atkins and wheat-free diets, but even when he was at his exercising peak, his abs never looked like the painter's. Maybe finishing the job will help him to lose a bit of weight. He needs to start something again. His belly looks like it's making up for lost time. It protrudes enough to rest a drink on now. There should be a six pack in the fridge. Flora is sitting at the dining room table, sipping on her tea; she's too consumed by her phone to speak to him. After the scene that played out with the painter, he's relieved to walk into silence.

The array of condiments in the fridge is so plentiful that he can't see any food. Jennifer had a thing for sauces: sweet chili, peri-peri, lemon and herb, coriander and thyme, tomato, mayonnaise and an assortment of mustard. It used to drive him mad.

He shifts a few things around and spots some leftover pizza.

It's a risk to open any container from the fridge. Flora won't throw anything away, even if there's a spoonful of rice left in the pot, she'll put it into a Tupperware and into the fridge, where it will stay until it transforms into a more alive and pungent version of itself.

The pizza still looks and smells like pizza.

"Do you need help, sir?" Flora hasn't looked up from her phone.

"No thanks, Flora." He doesn't want to disturb her when she's frantically messaging someone but he can't find the beer. "Actually, Flora, have you seen the beer?"

"It's finished, sir."

"Impossible. I bought some yesterday. They were just..."

"I found the empty bottles by the bin this morning."

"All six bottles? Who drank them?"

"I don't know, sir." She is finally looking at him. She has gotten older. Flora was young and vibrant when she started working for them. Now there's something about her eyes that looks strained. What must it have been like for her to have lived with them through Jennifer's illness, and now after her death?

"Can I warm the pizza for you?"

"No thanks. It's fine." Jennifer couldn't stand eating cold food and wouldn't let Frank do it either. "Do you want a slice Flora?"

She laughs and shakes her head but he's not sure if it's at him or her phone. He hasn't heard her laugh in a long time; it's strangely big for her small body.

"You sure?" She looks up at him and shakes her head. Her smile is gone.

He takes the pizza box back to the couch. The cricket has been rained out. The commentators discuss the chances of the game continuing. He eats the three slices of cold pizza.

"Dad, can I have some money?" Cathleen stands in the doorway. She shifts from one foot to the other.

"Hey sweetheart, sorry I think all the cash I had was in that jar."

She looks frustrated and bites at her bottom lip.

"Can't you go and draw some for me...Please?"

"Cath, I gave you money yesterday. Why don't you stay home tonight? We could watch a movie together."

"Dad, you gave me two hundred rand. How long do you expect that to last? Please, I already made plans with my friends."

She's wearing a skirt that's too small.

"Go and get changed darling. That skirt, it...it gives the wrong impression."

"I can't go anywhere without money, Dad." She stops her side-stepping and squares her body toward him. "Don't you have anything in your wallet?"

He hasn't told her that he's lost his job, a forced retirement. After Jennifer's death he fell to pieces. With his constant lateness and the smell of alcohol that hovered around him, they said they had to let him go. He's been hoping to find something else before needing to say anything to the kids. "There might be something. Go and fetch it from my bedroom."

She runs off, half of her bum hanging out of her skirt. "And please change, honey." She comes back down in the same excuse for a skirt and tosses the wallet at him. He opens it up. There's not much. He hands her a hundred rand note.

"Thanks Dad...isn't there any more?"

He gives her another fifty. That only leaves fifty for him. "Please will you change now?"

"It's fine, Dad. Just leave it."

"You might want to think about getting a part-time job." She closes her eyes. Perhaps it's too soon to suggest it. It's not the right way to have this conversation.

"Mom always said I should finish university without distractions."

"You're not studying this year."

"Dad, I told you that I'm not ready to go back yet. Why don't you ever listen to me!"

He nods. He's not in the mood for another confrontation.

"So, where's the hip happening spot tonight?"

She sighs at him and leaves.

# 6

# FARHANA
*Twenty-two with dimples deep enough to hold secrets*

Only during Ramsaan can time move this slowly. The ornate gold-rimmed clock in the dining room shows that there are still fifteen minutes before they can break their fast. The table is set. Two serving plates of rice bookend the table. The center is filled with three different types of curry—two chicken and one mutton—and masala steak, on hot trays, rotis, dal, atchar, pies and of course dates. She hates dates. They're fleshy and moist but that's what the prophet ate after he fasted so they pretend to ignore the more mouth-watering dishes on the overloaded table and mimic his ways.

"Farhana, the samoosas are ready."

She doesn't understand how her mother can cook while she's fasting. The smell is enough to make Farhana want to apply lip gloss just so that she can lick it off again. Lip gloss is not allowed until Eid.

Her mother is a round woman but her full cheeks have started to sag during this month when everyone starts looking gaunt. The maroon semicircles under her eyes make Farhana wish that her mother would cheat and at least taste the food as she cooks.

"Is that all, Mummy?"

"Yes, it's almost time. Tell everyone to wash up now."

"Gee, Mummy."

There's no need to tell anyone anything. Her entire gray family has been collectively staring at the clock. Washing has given them something to do, in an attempt to help the gold minute hand move along a little faster. A small queue has formed along the passage to the bathroom. She squeezes between two of her aunts, who somehow have the energy to be laughing about someone that Farhana's never heard of. She smiles at them as she takes the samoosas into the dining room. Her stomach flips. She's been feeling nauseous for most of Ramsaan but the feeling disappears after a few deep breaths.

She places the plate on the crowded table, around which some of the freshly-washed family are already seated, waiting for the final countdown. Her mother enters and there's a silence holding the suspense in the room. One by one the rest enter the dining room. Her aunts have stopped laughing. During Ramsaan, Farhana's mother puts a plastic table at the end of the wooden one to make sure there's enough space for everyone. All twenty of them are now sitting, elbows rubbing against each other. They are rigid, avoiding any noise that might distract them from hearing the Azaan ring out.

And then it comes as a melodious break in the tension.

*Allahu Akbar*
*Allahu Akbar*
*Allahu Akbar*
*Allahu Akbar*
*Ash-hadu al-la ilaha illa llah ...*

She looks around and everyone is mouthing the dua before break-ing the fast. Their mouths are moving at such a speed, you would think they were racing. Except for her Uncle Samad. He's the scariest of the lot and the most outwardly religious. He emphasizes each Arabic syllable of the prayer, making his thick graying beard bob between the air and his chest as a proclamation of his faith. He is best friends with the Molana at the mosque down the road and believes that he knows best when it comes to the Qur'an.

He pours himself a glass of water, then picks up a date and tosses it into his mouth.

Working out how to avoid eating dates during Ramsaan is like an anorexic trying to avoid a psychologist's eyes. Her feared uncle, who happens to be sitting directly opposite her, hands her the plate of dates. She takes one and looks around to find a place to discard it. She looks back at him. His eyes are still on her. He must know. Why else would anyone stare at someone holding a date? It's like he's daring her to throw it away—to waste food in the time when they are supposed to remember those without. She smiles with tight lips and moves the squishy horror toward her mouth. He's still watching her. What's wrong with him? He is purposefully torturing her. She's almost certain that her face is a total grimace but she slowly pushes it into her mouth. He smiles and starts to dish up. She grabs a serviette and stows the sticky monstrosity away.

"Please pass the butter chicken." She needs something to change the taste in her mouth. The nauseous feeling returns. She closes her eyes and breathes it away.

Creamy chicken, a fresh roti and a bit of mango atchar make her plate a faster's feast. She takes in the beauty before her and begins to eat.

What a mistake! The combination of the creamy chicken, the ghee from the roti, and the chili, combined with her date-flavored mouth is just too much. Bile rises in her throat. She swallows hard. Her stomach doubles over. She closes her eyes and prays for the feeling to go away. But the food keeps coming up. She stands to run to the bathroom but it's too late. Bits and pieces from sehri this morning explode out of her and land on the well-laid table. There are carrots in the mix. Why are there carrots in the mix?

Chairs are scraped backwards, away from the table. There are twenty pairs of eyes on her. Some are covering their mouths and noses. Others shake their heads. And some are shocked into stillness. Everything has been spoiled. The vomit reached almost every dish. If only she had been sitting at the end with the rice, maybe she would have been able to keep it contained in one bowl. She manages to stumble to the bathroom to escape her infringement of the rules of Iftar. She can't stop crying and her throat is sore from having to reverse its normal action.

"Farhana, are you okay?" Her mother's voice coaxes her to open the door.

She stands in front of her mother, still trembling. She doesn't want to go back out there. "I'm sorry."

Her mother hugs her tightly, enveloping the smell of vomit with flour, hot oil and spices. "Come and help to clean up. I will make a plan in the kitchen."

The bags under her mother's eyes seem to turn two shades darker as she speaks to her but her smile is reassuring. Farhana goes back into the bathroom and closes the door. She brushes her teeth and washes her face before heading back to the dining room.

Farhana keeps her head down and tries to focus on clearing the plates but she can feel the tears starting to build. The family is polite enough not to say anything but they're all starving and she's sure they must be angry. She knows better than to mess with anyone who has been fasting all day.

Her bearded uncle walks toward her. He looks like he's about to quote some religious story to her, or tell her what the prophet would have done. She doesn't want to hear it. If it wasn't for him and his stupid dates, none of this would have happened.

"Go and take a shower my child. We can handle this." She never noticed how his head nodded out his words before. He takes the wet cloth from her hand and continues to wipe the table.

"Come on, go now." His voice is suddenly stern and gets her moving swiftly. There's vomit in her hair. Maybe he wasn't trying to be nice at all and just wanted to get rid of her smell. "It'll help you feel better."

The shower is calming. She stands, surrounded by tiny white tiles, until the water starts to turn cold. She will have to deal with the shouting for that later.

The family is all in the lounge with plates on their laps. Toasted cheese and tomato for Iftar has surprisingly done the trick.

"Next time you must rather say that you don't feel like curry. This is much easier for your mother to make." Uncle Samad has everyone chuckling and Farhana's mother is laughing so hard that her chair is shaking. "So what do you feel like for tomorrow night Farhana? You must let your mother know early if she must buy more bread. Your cousin Husain has already eaten two sandwiches."

She smiles at her uncle. With food in their stomachs, the family has returned to normal. Everyone is relaxed and she can eat her toasted cheese in peace.

"Anyone for tea or coffee?" A mixture of responses has her flip into super-waitress mode. She wishes her mother would let her just bring a tray with the milk and sugar but her mother always insists that she serves everyone exactly what they want. They all speak at once, leaving her with a total of twelve teas and five coffees. Husain is happy drinking Fanta Grape. Three of the teas are rooibos, one with no sugar or milk, one with a bit of each and one with honey. Those wanting Ceylon make it easier—all five want two sugars and milk. The remaining four are masala teas, which her mother will make on the stove. Then there are the coffees, one with two sweeteners and no milk, one with one sweetener and milk, one with three sugars and a dash of milk, one with one sugar and lots of milk and finally her Uncle Samad who says that anything is fine. How can anything be fine? Everyone else has been specific; she knows how to give them what they want. Why must he be so very difficult? Is this some strange test? Why would he test her now of all times? She can't afford to make any more mistakes tonight, especially because she wants to go out later, which isn't really allowed during Ramsaan.

She goes to the kitchen, fills the kettle with water, switches it on and prepares the cups for the special orders. She still doesn't have a clue what to make for her uncle. She could just take him a glass of water; it was what the Prophet Mohamed drank. Her mother comes into the kitchen to make the masala tea.

"Mummy, what do you think Uncle Samad wants to drink?"

"Coffee, one sugar and milk. Just like Daddy used to have it."

She feels like crying again. Her father died five years ago, but she can't remember how he liked his coffee. She struggles to remember what his voice sounded like. She blows her nose on a paper towel and tries to focus on the hot beverages. She makes sure Uncle Samad is the first to get his. His beard smiles at her.

After everyone has had their drinks, people start to leave. Jackets, coats and scarves ready them for the world outside.

Farhana and her mother collect all the dishes and start the cleaning up process. There are dishes lined up for days on the different surfaces in the small pink kitchen. She rolls up her sleeves and sorts out the glasses and the crockery as the water fills the sink with bubbles. One at a time, they come out clean and shiny.

Her mother chose pink paint for the kitchen. She said she wanted it to be bright and cheerful. Farhana's father brought home a light pink, not the bright shade that her mother had hoped for.

Her mother never complained.

As Farhana reaches her hands into the soapy water, she sees the similarities between her hands and her mother's. Farhana's skin is a shade or two lighter but they have the same shape—short stubby fingers attached to circular palms. She wipes a plate that has three groups of flowers painted inside a brown border. These are the oldest plates in the house. Farhana loves them. When she was a child she would fight to make sure she was seated in front of one before any meal. Even now, when she makes food for herself, she will choose one of these plates.

Her mother is fast asleep on the couch when she returns to the lounge. She looks peaceful. Her mother loves falling asleep on the couch. She says that if she sleeps while the news is on, she gets the information unconsciously and gets to rest at the same time.

Farhana rubs her mother's arm gently and she wakes with a fright. The news these days is enough to give anyone nightmares.

"Mummy. Sorry, you want to go lie down in bed?"

Her mother moves in slow motion. Lifting her body like it's twice the size.

"Is it okay if I go out for a little while?"

Her mother's mouth starts to form an argument.

"I'm going with Tasneem and her brother to Rosebank for coffee. I won't be back late. Promise."

Her mother's exhaustion lets Farhana win. Her mother nods softly before she leaves Farhana and goes to her bedroom.

Farhana's phone buzzes. It's Zee. He wants to know if she can go out. Apparently there's a massive party in town tonight. With Zee, there's always a massive party.

I'm in. Mum's just gone 2 bed. Cum thru. x, she texts and rushes to her room. At least she's already showered. It'll take him just under half an hour to get to her, just enough time for clothes, hair and make-up. She likes to look good when she goes out with Zee. She isn't very experienced in the boyfriend department and this is turning out to be her most serious relationship so far.

A tightly-fitted purple dress, which she convinced her mum was a top, paired with her peep-toe ankle boots, gives her the right kind of edge for a town party. She runs a straightener through her already straight hair to remove a few slight signs of kink and goes a little wild on the make-up: dark eyes, rosy cheeks and glossy pink lips.

She sneaks to the bathroom to get a look in the long mirror.

The result is not what she was hoping for. The dress is pulling at the seams, especially around her waist. She thought that fasting would be a quick diet. The make-up is too heavy for her face. She has large features and this much color makes her look like a drag queen.

A hooter beeps three times. She wipes her face with some toilet paper but it's too late for her to change and she really doesn't want her mother to wake up and find her dressed like this—or worse, to see Zee. She grabs her phone, handbag and house keys, and heads out to the red Citi Golf parked a little way up the street.

She opens the door and jumps in.

"Hey babe. You don't want to bring a jacket?" She feels his eyes on the extra weight around her center.

"It'll be hot inside. I'm fine." She attempts to be nonchalant.

"You look great."

She's certain he's lying.

She sees Lenasia, the familiar mixture of differently-sized houses, speed past her window.

Next year is going to be incredible. Zee says that his parents are going to get him a new car. He's not sure what kind exactly but she's hoping for a silver BMW 135i with tinted windows. He slows down at a stop street, next to a squat-face brick house that looks as though it is peering up at its double-story pillared neighbor. They're around the corner from the quiet road where they usually stop. Living with your parents makes you explore the city for special spots of privacy.

"Babe, did I tell you? It looks like I'm going to be getting my own place soon. It's going to be killer. Probably somewhere in Newtown. I went to check out a few spots close to the Mandela Bridge. That's where it's all happening."

He passes the turn for their road. "Do you mind if we skip it tonight? Don't have much time. Have to meet up with some people."

She does mind. It feels like rejection.

"Please can we stop? It feels like it's been so long. I miss you."

She tries her best to look sexy.

"Of course, I was kidding babe." He laughs.

He turns the car around and stops in the cul-de-sac. She jumps into the back seat.

Her cousin told her that rich boys need extra encouragement to keep driving out to Lenz and she doesn't plan on losing Zee before he gets that apartment. They'll finally have a space to be alone in and it's so close to Wits, they would have more time together.

They start kissing. He's gentle with her.

She runs her hand down his chest. He's skinny and she can feel his ribcage. She's jealous of his petite and lean body, perfect for skinny jeans. Her fingers trace along the length of his prominent forehead and fall into his manicured dreadlocks.

Their kissing becomes more intense, tongues battling each other for space. He pulls back and stares at her. It's uncomfortable. She doesn't know where to look or how to be. She closes her eyes and moves toward him with too much force, smacking his mouth with her chin. She wants to cry but tries to laugh it off.

"You okay?" He strokes her chin. "Super eager today, aren't you?"

"I'm sorry. I'm fine, I just..."

He kisses her chin with small pecks. He looks young from this angle, like a baby animal suckling at its mother. She pulls away and faces forward.

"Do you want to go?" He looks momentarily hurt.

"No, no. I just need a minute, sorry."

She keeps her eyes wide and moves to kiss him. He wraps his arms around her and pulls her close to him. The smells of the car, cigarettes, weed and his spicy deodorant combine into a strange off-putting combination.

He runs his fingers along her back and they settle above her hips. Can he feel that she's getting fatter?

She moves his hands sharply, onto her breasts. It's not a bad thing that they're a little bigger.

Then she moves her hands down to his lap. His hardness always shocks her. Her fingers struggle with his button. Why is the hole so small? She moves the button backwards and forwards but can't get it out. Eventually he undoes it with two fingers.

The back seat of the car is constricting. He shimmies his bum out of his jeans with enormous difficulty and then crouches with his back facing her and peels the jeans down past his bent knees. She is pressed up against the window, trying to give him as much space as possible. Finally he shuffles around to face her. She can see his penis. It's long and thin like the rest of him. She tries not to be, but every time she sees it she is surprised.

He rolls her dress up to her waist and she lies down on the seat. He straddles her and removes her panties, with great effort. She needs to make a plan to get some sexier underwear but her mother is always with her.

Eventually, his body straightens over her and his weight releases. Luckily he's not a heavy guy.

"Shit!"

"What? What's wrong?"

"The condom's in the back pocket of my jeans."

"We can do the pull-out thing if you want?"

"That's only for when we don't have condoms, babes."

They start laughing as they renegotiate the space, both of them trying to reach the pocket.

At last they find the condom, open it and roll it on. Zee uses his hand to insert himself inside her. They get into a rhythm. He moves her hair out of her face and looks into her eyes. His smile is full and warm and he tells her that she's exceptional. The thrusts get harder and faster. For a moment, she imagines them in his new loft apartment—high ceilings and an arty open-plan design with loads of space. She will decorate with a hint of the seventies. They will have it all—waking up in the loft, then heading out for breakfast in the new BMW. They're both excited. His hand pushes down on her shoulder as he readies himself for the finale, and then drops into awkward little shudders. She smiles at him and their future.

He sits up and starts to get dressed again but keeps lifting his eyes to meet hers. There is something different happening to his face; he seems insecure, or scared, even.

"Are you okay?"

He stops fussing and stares at her. "I'm...yes, fine...happy. You ready to go?"

His face is close to hers and she nods.

"Good. Still have to pick up the party favors for tonight." He jumps over, back into the driver's seat.

She finds her underwear under the passenger seat and joins him in the front. The car groans into action and they're back on the road.

He holds her hand when he doesn't need to change gears.

She loves the highway. The lights, the speed, and the deep house music playing on the radio are great companions for the journey toward the north of Johannesburg. As soon as they pass the old gold mines, everything starts to get bigger. The buildings tower above them. One day she will work for a firm in one of those high-rises.

Zee takes a turn-off from the highway. The buildings are still tall but become decrepit, the spectacular light disappears and they enter Hillbrow.

She hates this part of the night. Her jaw tightens as he stops and turns off the lights of the car.

"I won't be long." He kisses her gently. She wraps her arms around her body as he opens the door and locks her in. She should have brought a jacket. This is not a deserted street; clusters of people approach the car from different directions. Each group that heads toward the car has her squeeze herself tighter, her arms encasing her body like a spring roll. It's a futile attempt to disappear. As the groups pass the car, she rubs her body gently, attempting to soothe herself before more suspects head her way.

She plays different games in her mind in order to keep sane. Seeing how many times she can press each finger into its counterpart on the opposite hand in a minute usually helps. After only five touches, she sees a single man in the rear-view mirror. He seems to be checking out the car. From where he is standing, he won't know that she's sitting inside. Golfs are high on the theft and hijacking list. Uncle Samad was recently saying that was the reason he didn't buy one. The man is getting closer to the car. His body seems relaxed but his strides have definitely picked up pace. He pulls something out of his pocket but she can't make out what it is.

The door opens and her heart sinks.

"Those guys up there are ridiculous. You should come up with me one day. They're hilarious." Zee gets into the car. "Sorry I took so long, babes. It's tough to leave when they're mid-story."

In the rear-view mirror she sees the man putting his key into the front door of a building. She wonders if he was as scared as she was, questioning why this car was parked in front of his doorway.

She sighs heavily.

"You okay?"

"It's fine. I'm fine. Just start the car." She moves as close to him as the seatbelt and gearbox will allow. "So what did you get?" Her shoulders have relaxed but her eyes haven't stopped darting around.

He's still not driving. She wants to lean over and force his foot down onto the accelerator.

"It was a fuck-up. He only had twelve grams of coke but I got some pills as well. You think you might try something?"

"Maybe later." They have this conversation regularly but both of them know that she won't take anything. Every time she sees the drugs, she thinks of Cathleen. The only thing that has her a little curious is that it looks like a great diet plan. Cathleen is half the size that she was when they first met. Besides the weight, Cathleen is a walking anti-drug campaign and after seeing some of the things that Cathleen does when she's high, Farhana swore never to touch the stuff.

Thank goodness! They're almost at Jan Smuts Avenue.

Zee's phone beeps. He picks it up.

"It's from Cathleen. She'll be there in an hour or so. It's going to be a great night. Got my first sell and we're not even there yet. Maybe I can get you those jeans you want." He strokes her leg. She adores presents. "You should have been there last night."

She hates it when he says that. It's selfish. He knows that she depends on him to get around.

"I didn't know anything was happening last night." She attempts to keep accusation out of her voice. It's too difficult for her to go out during the week, anyway. Her mother would never allow it, especially not during Ramsaan.

"It was totally last minute. The music was sick. Some DJ from Norway, I think." His version of an apology always sounds like an excuse. "Cath was off the rails, she left with some random. It looks like tonight is going to be better."

The road is full and they turn down one of the side alleys to find parking. They head toward the entrance. Zee is a stride ahead of her. Her heels beat against the uneven road in an effort to keep up. Once they get to the main road they part ways; he heads out to make sales while she goes inside. It will take him around twenty minutes before he joins her.

The girl at the door takes Farhana's money and stamps the inside of her wrist. The first time she got stamped, she was terrified that her mother would see traces of ink, and scrubbed her arm raw as soon as she got home.

She starts her twenty minute routine. She has a cigarette and a walkabout to see if there are any familiar faces, then stops in to the bathroom to check her hair and make-up and faff about as much as possible, then to the bar to place their order....It usually takes the barman at least five minutes to notice her. By the time the drinks are in her hand, Zee is by her side, paying the man.

He managed to sell it all but kept a little coke for Cathleen.

Farhana has a sip of the cheap red wine. Most people don't drink wine at places like this but she thinks it's classy. She only needs one glass to feel the effects. Zee orders two tequilas. Lemon and salt are essential for her; he takes his straight.

Her stomach has an immediate reaction to the acid. She takes a big gulp of wine in an attempt to hold the tequila down. She wants to vomit again.

Zee drags her outside. "You're soaking wet."

It's true. Sweat speeds down her forehead. Zee struggles to wipe it away.

"Babe, you don't look good. Come, I'll take you home."

She can't argue. He helps her across the street.

"Hey Zee. Are you guys leaving already? Hanna, you look like shit!" It's Cathleen.

"It's Farrrr-hana." She can only manage a whisper.

"Yeah, we're out Cath. Later." Zee pulls Farhana to the car.

"Wait. Zee." Cathleen looks uncharacteristically insecure. "You have anything?"

"Pay me later. Enjoy." Zee slips his hand into his pocket. He grabs a small plastic bag and tosses it to Cathleen.

Why does Zee always give Cathleen free crap? He hardly ever makes her pay full price. Maybe Cathleen uses other ways to pay Zee. She tends to be strangely intimate with Zee, often touching him on the shoulder and calling him at whatever time of the night she feels like it. Farhana doesn't know what happens between the two of them when she's not around. She used to speak to Zee about it. He said that they're family friends. She had to let it go because her jealousy makes Zee angry. She's feeling too ill right now to fight.

# 7

# FLORA
*It only there was more*

When she closes her eyes, his smell surrounds her. It is a wondrous combined smell. Something between the freshness of a newly peeled orange and the sharp acidity of paint remover bends inside her. It coaxes her body into relaxing and her breathing slows. She's scared that this smell won't last unless she sees him again. Dark skin and shoulders broadened by hard work made her shy when she took him his tea. Her eyes were shy, only meeting his for a few seconds before diverting her gaze back to the floor. But her nose bravely took all of him in.

The first time their fingers touched was during one of the regular tea exchanges. She expected to feel leather but he must be using the lotion that makes those white ladies dance on TV.

After that she became strategic in the way that she held his cup to make sure that she would not miss out on any opportunity to feel his softness.

She started wearing nicer clothes to work in, waking up a bit earlier to spend time on herself. Today she wore her long maroon church skirt with a soft blouse. It was nearly impossible to scrub the floors and she was irritated that he had her behaving like a young girl. He was causing havoc with her schedule.

When he left, she had to stop herself from chasing after him to ask for his shirt. She would have never washed that shirt. It would have stayed on her pillow right next to her nose. But she didn't ask. She didn't move at all. She just stood there staring at him through the window.

His face struggled to remain calm during the accusations.

None of them knew that she was watching. His mouth twitched but he stayed true to his silence.

She was too unsettled to concern herself with anything for the rest of the day. She didn't even care when James put on a horror movie while she was babysitting, earlier this evening. Usually she would have made a big fuss and would've forced him to watch something else. All that blood and dead people running around trying to kill other people, it was disgusting. It's not good for children to watch these things, it infests their brain with the devil's work. These movies are one of the reasons for Cathleen's behavior. Cathleen was lovely as a small girl. She and Zilindile used to play for hours in the garden, making up games and taking turns at bossing each other around. She had seemed to be growing up well, always had her nose in this or that book. As soon as she finished a book, she would give Flora all the details. And Cathleen read well, she could answer all of Flora's questions about the characters and why they did certain things.

When Mrs. Joseph came home with new books, Flora was thrilled. Cathleen would be telling her new stories in no time. The books and the stories are both gone. Flora and Cathleen have nothing more to talk about. Flora can occasionally manage to convince James to at least watch movies about love, or a nice comedy. This way she knows that he is getting good messages from the TV. But earlier this evening, she had allowed him to do what he wanted.

She hears footsteps approach her door. They are stumbling and un-even as though the person is a cripple. A thud against the door makes her sit upright. All she can think of are the zombies from that stupid movie. What nonsense! Her ears open wide, searching for the calming chime of keys. The person outside staggers; she hears their feet take numerous steps. Have they fallen? There is now silence.

The person could be sorting out the variety of tools they brought with them, to torture her with. Her body is still at a rigid ninety degree angle but her hands won't stop trembling.

The bedside lamp starts to look like a perfect weapon. The long metallic stand has the potential to inflict some harm and the lampshade won't be hard to replace. She shifts her body toward it as quietly as possible, inching over, millimeters at a time. Her fingers shake as she attempts to grab at the plug. She lets go as she hears that wondrous sound: the jingle of keys. They hit around the keyhole until one finds its way inside.

A gasp escapes from her mouth. She lies back down and moves to-ward the edge of her single bed, closest to the wall. It is only Zilindile. These horror movies are bad news! If they give her mind so many crazy ideas, imagine what poor James is dreaming about.

Zilindile is making an effort to be quiet but knocks into the sink and falls backwards onto her favorite chair.

Mrs. Joseph hated that chair and was always complaining that it was tacky but Flora loves it. She loved it from the moment that Mr. Joseph brought it home. The emerald green fabric with pink butterflies makes her feel like she's sitting on a picnic. After it got one little stain, it became Flora's. Red grape juice always makes her smile now. She hopes Zilindile hasn't broken it but she hates speaking to him when he's like this. For a good boy, he can get really rude.

She pretends to sleep and ignores the horse kicking around in the room. Finally he manages to take off his shoes and clothes and gets into bed. He sleeps on a mattress next to her bed. The stench of a she-been climbs up the side of her bed and joins her underneath Cathleen's old "Under the Sea" duvet. She shuffles as close to the wall as she can get but the smell crawls all over her.

Zilindile has no trouble falling asleep and is snoring like a little bee. She prays that tonight his dreams will tell him to join the church. She can always rest better when he's home but she needs to take him away from these people and their bad influences.

When Mrs. Joseph was around, this was the ideal environment to raise a child. Flora thought that it would give Zilindile opportunities. There was a promise to send him to university after matric. There's no point anymore.

She peeps at him over the side of the bed. He is peaceful. Now that he is home, she can drift off to sleep. Her eyelids are heavy and she frowns as her phone starts beeping. Her mouth stretches into a yawn and she turns off the alarm. It's still dark but between the cold creeping in from under her door and the smell coming off Zilindile, which has filled the room, she's up.

She wraps a towel around her nightie and gets her things together for the shower. The room is cold but when she pushes the door open, the chill is worse than standing in front of an open fridge. She rushes toward the bathroom and dances along the cracked tiles as she waits for the water to warm up.

Clean and ready for the day, she walks along the half-painted wall to the big house. Part of Runyararo's scent is still present. Her body wants to hug the wall. This is ridiculous. Who would want a man with a crowded market place in his mouth? She wants to be sensible but her finger runs along the wall like a teenager until it reaches the area still awaiting his magical paint.

It won't come. He's gone.

He wasn't a thief. She knows a tsotsi when she sees one. No one that smells so good would steal.

She should have said something, but things only started to go missing when Zilindile finished school. Zilindile always has new clothes, petrol money and plenty of airtime. She is not such a fool to think you can get that kind of money from working at a bar. Mr. Joseph hasn't noticed half of the things that have gone missing. If the madam was still around, it would've been spotted immediately.

The madam organized this house and knew what goes where. This caused many fights for Flora. Mrs. Joseph had no sense of style but would never take advice from Flora. There was a beautiful pink vase that Mrs. Joseph wanted hidden. Every day Flora would take out the vase and place it on the dining room table. While Flora was busy, getting flowers in the garden, Mrs. Joseph would pack it away again. That vase didn't know if it was coming or going. It's one of the items that have gone missing. It drives Flora mad because there's no one to put it back into the cupboard anymore.

Flora has rearranged the house and it is a marked improvement.

Mr. Joseph hasn't noticed a thing.

Flora reaches the back door at the same time as Cathleen. This is what happens to children without mothers. Only coming home with the sun!

"It is morning, Cathy."

Cathleen stares at Flora silently.

What a disgraceful child. Flora used to change her nappies and now she can't even say hello.

A blank stare from baggy eyes is all she gets.

"Getting home at this hour? You must be careful. It's not nice for a girl to be out that late."

"You be careful! Remember who you work for!" Cathleen has turned cold like one of the zombies in the movie.

"What would your mother say?" Flora moves past Cathleen and turns on the kettle.

"Oh, leave me alone!" Cathleen slinks off to her bedroom.

"If you continue like this, you're going to get AIDS. The way you look these days, I wouldn't be surprised if you already have it." Flora says, speaking to no one at all.

There's time for a quick game of *Snake 2* while she waits for the kettle to boil. Her snake is growing. She chases after the flickering dots. She's on fast speed and her snake eats and eats. It bites itself and she's dead.

"Morning Flora." Mr. Joseph drags himself past her and starts making himself a cup of coffee.

"Morning, sir." There is only enough water in the kettle for one cup.

"Flor, have you seen my blue bag?" James is shouting from the bottom of the stairs.

"Which one, James?" She sees Mr. Joseph pour the water into his cup and place the kettle back on its stand without refilling it. He leans back against the kitchen counter.

"The one with my cricket stuff." Flora follows James upstairs to look. The bag is in a corner of his room under a pile of dirty clothes.

"James, come on already. You told me you need to be at school early. I'm up now so will you please hurry up!" Mr. Joseph is shouting from the kitchen doorway. "Flora where are the car keys?"

She is rushing back down the stairs when she sees the keys on the banister. She has not yet made James's lunch. She hands Mr. Joseph the keys and dashes into the kitchen. There are only two slices of bread left. Mr. Joseph paces up and down in the kitchen. Flora is out of breath as she makes a peanut butter and jam sandwich and takes out four Provitas and layers them with cheese. Mr. Joseph is muttering to himself.

"Where is this boy? James!"

"I'm here, Dad."

"Good, let's go."

"Bye, Flor." James grabs his lunch and follows his father outside.

This new hairstyle of James's is crazy. It looks like he doesn't own a comb but she's seen how long it takes him to make it look like that so she doesn't say anything. What must the teachers be thinking? These children are too young to be so concerned with their looks.

She fills the kettle and waits for it to boil. Runyararo is probably at home, having to make his own tea.

One more game, while she has her tea. Her fingers are good enough to play with one hand. The score is adding up and she's about to beat her own record. She has to focus completely and places the cup down but it misses the table and crashes to the floor.

The snake dies. She cleans up the broken pieces of porcelain and wipes up the tea.

Fortunately Mr. Joseph won't notice.

She fills the sink with water and Sunlight and lines up the dishes.

One more game before she washes them. Her snake dies too quickly.

That game doesn't count. One more try. Her thumb is the boss of her phone. The snake dies again. It's time to start washing. Cathleen only comes down from her room after lunchtime. It doesn't look like she's washed. She leaves without saying anything. It's unbelievable that the girl has managed to make such a mess since yesterday. If she was Flora's daughter, she would at least have to make her own bed. These children are spoiled. Flora has helped to spoil them. James is only slightly better than Cathleen but he is still a small boy. What will

Cathleen do when she gets married? She can't cook or clean. Who will marry such a girl?

Flora picks up the clean clothes from the floor and packs them into the cupboard. You don't need to be a detective to work out which clothes are dirty; the smell of smoke is strong and she doesn't need to bring them close to her face to be sure. Before putting them in the laundry basket, she empties Cathleen's pockets. There's always money rolled into tubes.

She makes the bed. An old family album falls out when she shakes the duvet. It is Cathleen's baby album, filled with photographs of Cathleen and Mr. and Mrs. Joseph. Flora remembers that time but there are no photographs of her in the album.

The sheets have brown stains from Cathleen's feet but she will have to live with them for the weekend. Today is Flora's early day. She won't be doing the bedding.

She walks downstairs and sits on the couch while she waits for James to come home. There's time to play her game without any distractions. The snake moves across the screen.

Runyararo's face is clear in her mind, thick slightly-cracked lips and soft eyes that are a finger too far apart. She wishes she could force the image to smile but it remains hard.

If she could prove that Zilindile is the thief then she might be able to get Runyararo his job back. She would make Zilindile replace everything and explain to Mr. Joseph that he is just a child going through some difficulties. Mr. Joseph should understand, with Cathleen being no better right now.

Perhaps it was Cathleen. She wouldn't put it past her.

Mind you, Cathleen gets money from her father all the time. It probably adds up to more than Flora's wages. She wouldn't have to bother with stealing. You have to know where to sell things and Cathleen looks too scared of anything that looks like work.

Zilindile is the only one with street smarts. But if Flora tells Mr. Joseph, he might kick Zilindile out or call the police. She could say that she found the money under the couch or behind the cabinet but she doesn't know how much was stolen. She will have to trap Zilindile in the act and force him to tell her.

The snake has filled up the screen.

The doorbell rings.

"Hi Flor, it's me." Flora opens the door. James has two big bags weighing down his shoulders. Why must these children carry all this around? Flora doubts they can use that much in one day. He drops the bags at the bottom of the staircase.

"Hello boy. You want something to eat?"

"Ja, I'm starving. Please can I have two hotdogs?" He follows her into the kitchen. "So, you beat my high score yet?" A cheeky grin spreads across his face.

"Ooooh James, I played so well today. Hmmm. You should have seen my snake go." She takes two rolls out of the freezer and puts them into the microwave to defrost. James sits on the counter next to her.

"Ja, but did you beat my score?"

"No. Yours is still the top score but tomorrow I will play the whole day and then my score will be the highest."

"Then you'll have to give me my phone back so I can set the record straight." He picks up the phone and starts playing.

"You mean you don't have a snake on your fancy new phone?"

"No, I downloaded some awesome new games, though. Better than Snake!"

"But is it better than Snake 2?" They laugh.

Flora hands James his hotdogs, coated in tomato sauce the way he likes them, and they go and sit in front of the TV. He reaches for the remote.

"James, no zombies today. Shoo, you must have had such a bad sleep." They watch a show about a family. It's very funny but then she sees two men who are married to each other. Ag, TV is no good these days. This is worse than the zombies!

# 8

# CATHLEEN
*Clumps of hair block up the drain*

The cracks in the floor have formed in a haphazard fashion. There are so many that they almost form a map of a town that was never planned. She is sitting on a stained stool and the smell of disinfectant is rank. Bars are worse in the afternoon. The sunlight exposes the build-up of filth that the nighttime's mass of heaving bodies has not yet arrived to disguise. She's chain-smoking to block the chemical odor from penetrating her nostrils. There is no mystery here. This bar contains as much romance as B-grade porn. The only good thing is that she is happy not to have to talk to anyone.

There are only a handful of people inside. At a table across from Cathleen is a girl in cheap torn jeans that sit a bit too high on her body. They make her bum look like it starts opposite her belly-button. The long butt shifts from left to right and then perks up into the air like the perfect punctuation to her flirting.

The man she's with is old. His skin looks burnt and he has dark splotches on his cheeks. He seems to be enjoying her rear end. He strokes it and then looks over at Cathleen. He whispers something to the girl.

They both stare at Cathleen, while sipping their beers that are probably lukewarm by now. The woman breaks into a cackle. There's a tooth missing from her crooked smile.

Cathleen looks down at her whiskey. It's low and watery. She signals to the bartender for a top-up.

"What do we have here?" The voice comes from right behind her. It sounds familiar.

She swings around. It's horse-face.

"Hi Eddie." Her feet swirl her back to find a fresh drink. She's relieved and downs the double. Her hand taps the glass and the bartender refills it. Eddie places his hand on her shoulder and rubs his body against hers as he walks around to face her. He smells like a wet cigarette.

"Nice panties." She looks down. Her skirt has risen up around her waist like a belt.

She jumps off the plastic seat. Her thighs unglue themselves from the plastic with the speed of an expert bikini-waxer. She hurriedly pulls the skirt down over the red blotches on the backs of her legs. Maybe that's why the girl and her old man boyfriend were laughing at her.

"Hey where are you going?"

"To the bathroom."

"Can I join you?" Eddie taps his jacket pocket. "I've got some of the fun stuff."

"Fine, Eddie, fine. Just wait for like five minutes and then come. I have to pee first."

"Can't I watch?" A big stupid grin spreads across his face. She could take him. He's a scrawny guy, probably wouldn't be up too fast after a solid punch. There's something oddly soft about him. It would be easy to get the coke from him. Then she wouldn't have to hang around him either.

"Just kidding, angel tits, see you in five." He winks at her. It's like a bad eighties movie.

The floors are sticky and every step is like peeling off a post-it note. There's a faint smell of vomit lingering in the air. None of the stalls have working doors so she stretches out like Spiderman, one hand keeping the door closed and the other helping her to balance over the discolored toilet seat.

A door creaks open.

"Just a second, Eddie. I'm not done yet." The toilet paper is finished. She shakes her hips, trying to get as much of her piss off as possible.

"I'm no Eddie, darling." A gruff woman's voice replies.

The stall door is shoved open. Cathleen is knocked back and falls onto the toilet seat and then onto the sanitary bin, which spills open, exposing a strange combination of things along with the pads and tampons. An old lipstick rolls toward her foot and a hot-pink false nail falls out, pointing straight at the girl from the bar.

She moves toward Cathleen who is wedged into a corner where the bin used to be and whose shoulders squeeze up to her ears to avoid further contact with the toilet. The girl lifts her left foot and places it down on Cathleen's ribcage. She is pushed further into the corner. The floor is black and slightly moist. What is she sitting on?

"Give me the money darling."

"I don't have any cash on me."

The outside door opens.

"You better be ready for me." Eddie's voice has never sounded better.

He walks to the stall. The girl is not distracted, she continues to stare down at Cathleen.

"You want me to call Lionel?" Cathleen shakes her head, assuming Lionel is the old man. Eddie is standing right behind the girl now. Why is he not doing anything?

"Hey Dina, what's this about?"

She doesn't take her eyes off Cathleen.

Eddie knows her.

"She still hasn't paid from the last time. We thought she was going to leave it with the bartender. She kept looking at us and then at him like she was talking in code but he said she didn't give him nothing. Go call Lionel."

"You should have paid." Eddie turns to leave.

"What? I don't know them. Why do I owe them money?" She hears the door swing closed. "Please, please let me go. I'll get the money. How much is it? My dad will give it to me. I promise."

Her voice is shaking.

"We already gave you an extra day to pay. Lionel is not going to be happy. I'll tell you that for free." Cathleen can't move.

Dina pulls a cigarette out of the pocket of her jeans and lights it. She pulls hard and fast. She has a guttural cough that sounds like it's full of phlegm. Ash from the cigarette falls onto Cathleen.

"I thought girls like you were supposed to be smarter than this."

She takes a long drag of her cigarette, exposing fine lines around her lips. As she speaks, smoke comes out of her nose and mouth simultaneously. "You rich girls are all the same, trying to rip off people who are just trying to do a job. You should've asked Daddy for more cash."

The door swings open. The footsteps are heavy and precise. A man in a suit and a red tie stands in the doorway. His face is no longer blurred. It's not the old man. It's the man from the other morning.

# FLORA
*Stretched out fingers can get cut*

The white cotton dress, detailed with pink flowers along the neck-line, has been placed on the bed. She had her entire collection of dresses out before going to shower but the white one stood out. As she finishes putting on her lotion, she looks at it. It's perfect.

She's using a new lotion that she bought from the Spar around the corner, Nivea "Happy Blossoms." Lifting her arm up to her nose is like inhaling an entire garden. The smell is filling the room.

She slips into the dress and feels the weight of the cotton as the bottom hits the floor; it's too long to wear with flats so she gets her high heels out. They are black with a strap that ties around the ankle. She has only worn them a handful of times and they still look as good as new. She shines them up with a cloth, for an extra glow.

Her mirror is small. It used to be Mrs. Joseph's bathroom mirror. When they fixed up the bathroom a few years ago, the mirror was given to Flora. It's only big enough to show one section of her body at a time.

She looks at her face first. Her skin is not as firm as it once was and feels like it is getting thinner, worn away by time. The number of white hairs plaited into her bun is growing faster than she would like.

She tilts the mirror down to see the rest of her body. The dress is looking good. It makes her look like she has more of a figure than she really has.

When she was still a girl, she would get teased about her body. The lack of breasts and behind gave her a boyish look. The black school tunic did nothing to help her. It hung like a sack on a ruler. Her mother once caught her trying to stuff a dishtowel into the back of her panties. Her mother laughed so hard, she barely had a voice by the time the shouting for taking the cloth came.

Today, Flora doesn't need any foreign objects in her underwear.

The mirror shows the black tips peeping out from under her dress. The shoes aren't perfect but they're her only heels. They make her feel tall and elegant.

"Mama, are you getting married or something?" Zilindile is only coming home now. His eyes are blood red.

"I'm going to visit Aunty Sheryl. Why? What do you mean?"

He throws himself onto his mattress.

"That's not how you usually dress for a Saturday morning visit. It's too much. Where did you even get that dress from?"

"It was in the cupboard."

He has already turned over and passed out. His mouth is wide open like a hippo waiting for flies.

Next month she will buy herself a big mirror so that she can see herself properly.

Perhaps she should reconsider and wear the maroon skirt with a crisp white shirt—but that is too proper and church-like. What would happen if she bumped into Runyararo? He must have one of those life-altering realizations that happen in the movies. If he were drinking a juice, the sight of her would make him squeeze his drink into his mouth so fast, he would choke—just a little, not so much that it's dangerous. She would smile sweetly at him and rub his back. Her hands on the firm ridges of his back.

That would never happen if she is wearing a church outfit!

What does Zilindile know about grown-up fashion anyway? His idea of dressing up is wearing pants that are too small and shirts that hang off his body.

She grabs her handbag, some money and her phone.

The air outside creeps through the material of the dress and turns her whole body into chicken meat. She needs a jersey.

Zilindile doesn't notice the door opening and closing as Flora comes back inside.

She owns three jerseys: a bright red one, a black one with a zip and a beige one. Today is not the day to play it safe. She grabs the red one. It is soft and warm and seems to comfort her nerves.

She decides to put her tekkies on; it's quite a walk before she gets to the taxis. She puts her heels into a plastic bag and has one last glance at her face in the mirror. She is a woman today.

She starts her journey toward Jan Smuts Avenue. Her cheeks feel bruised from the cold. She pulls her red jersey up as high as it will go. The smell of paint from the house on her right makes her lips spread like a teenager.

What if Runyararo is working here? There are three guys that she can see working on the house but they all look young and she can hear they're South African. They probably wouldn't even know Runyararo. She keeps walking slowly, enjoying the scent for as long as she can.

She visits Sheryl in Hillbrow once a month. Runyararo also lives in Hillbrow. She wonders if he's found a new job yet. She knows the name of his building but it's a high-rise with hundreds of rooms. She doesn't know the number of his flat. If he is at home, he might never come outside. She could wait there the whole day.

This was a stupid idea. She should go straight to Sheryl's place and forget this whole thing but she doesn't want to give up entirely. She'll choose a route to walk past his place on the way to Sheryl's.

It was a good idea to wear the tekkies.

She reaches the corner of Jan Smuts and Westcliff Drive. A taxi stops right in front of another car, making the driver hoot and swear. She crosses the road quickly and jumps into a taxi that's waiting there. There's a space in the front. She loves sitting in the seat next to the driver. It makes her feel special, being up front, but she doesn't have the stress of having to count the money like the person in the passenger seat.

"Uyaphi Mama?"

Good question. Where is she going? What's a good stop that's not too far from his place to walk past there? She should have thought this through.

"Kotze Street." She says the first place that comes to mind.

The driver is so old that his wrinkles have wrinkles; he should be calling her Sisi not Mama! She pays him and gets her phone out. Her last game of *Snake 2* is still on pause. She's close to beating her high score. This is the best she's ever played. The snake is taking over the screen. She doesn't allow the jerking stop-starts of the taxi to distract her from maneuvering the tricky snake. The changing landscape next to the window is a blur.

"Kotze Street," the man alongside her pokes her in the ribs.

The taxi stops. Cockeyed gap-toothed buildings with fragmented windows that reflect the sunlight in a strangely welcoming way replace the leafy suburb of Parkview and all its barking dogs. Besides the mixture of rubbish there are also chunks of cement missing from the pavement. She would have broken her neck trying to navigate this place in her high heels. But her tekkies make her feel like she's on an adventure.

There are so many people on the streets on a Saturday that it's hard to see anything. She makes her way to a spaza shop. It's busy and she has to squeeze between two oversized ladies to get to the fridge. They have the kind of figures she has always dreamed of, watermelon behinds and drumstick thighs. One of the ladies is wearing an exquisitely decorated brown doek; the other has thick braids down to the middle of her back. The ladies are in the middle of a dramatic conversation about the husband of the lady with the doek.

How can they talk about such things in the middle of all these strangers? Flora grabs a coke and hears that the husband was caught fooling around. Apparently the woman walked into their home and found him at the height of his business with some skinny woman. The ladies give Flora's slender frame a good looking over, as she passes them on her way to the till, before they continue with the story.

Hillbrow suddenly feels too big. Looking into the eyes of the people walking past her, she wonders how many of them are on failed adventures of their own. Each of them is so full of thoughts and plans and dreams. Some walk with speed, in a rush to get to where they need to go. Others, mainly younger ones, bounce along as though they have nowhere to be.

They irritate her. Life has never been that easy.

She used to want it to be. When she met Paul, Zilindile's father, they were both young and nothing seemed to matter. They were in love and that was enough for them. Many days were spent laughing, without any worries. She walked slowly when she walked with him. He always made her late for work and would try to get her to leave early. He got her fired more than once.

Then she started working for the Joseph family. It was far away and they wanted her to stay on their property but Paul would visit regularly. She'd sneak him into the backroom for weeks at a time.

No one tells you that happiness like that doesn't last.

She's too old to deal with heartbreak again.

Her phone beeps. Sheryl has to go out and run some errands and wants to move their visit to the following week. Flora came here for nothing.

If she goes home now, Zilindile will start with the questions.

This was a stupid idea.

# 10

# RUNYARARO
*His mouth is full*

"Man, you are not going to believe what I have done for you!"

Shuvai is overjoyed. He is leaping around the barely-furnished single room. With a little more speed, he could run in circles along the wall with his spidery long legs.

Runyararo's eyes are patient, awaiting the big news. Shuvai is only ten years younger than him but today he has the energy of a fifteen-year-old.

"Man, this is big stuff! Major business this time!" Shuvai's hands keep gesturing toward the low ceiling like it's all too much for him.

Runyararo stares at him. He is waiting good-naturedly like a father whose child has just had an incredible day but still has no idea what the excitement is about.

"We should go out and celebrate, man. A nice cold beer. We should treat ourselves to the best of the best." Neither one of them really drinks beer. This really must be huge.

"You are going to love me for this one. We might be able to move out of this matchbox. Get a proper spot. It could even have a garden or whatever. Maybe somewhere in Yeoville. And it would only be us living there, man. We could have our own bedrooms. Imagine, a whole room to yourself. Hell, a whole house, with walls between the lounge and the kitchen."

He keeps emphasizing and the teeth keep smiling. Why can't he just spit it out? Runyararo has never had any reason not to trust Shuvai. Runyararo's face is frozen into a grin from a feeling that sits somewhere between pride for the man who has become like his younger brother, and his own boyish excitement as he loses himself in the smells and tastes that a real home promises. The things he could do in a kitchen! His mouth starts watering as he thinks about freshly-baked bread in the mornings. The possibility of a home and all that it will allow for feels like an excessive dream.

He still needs to think about sending money to Zimbabwe for his family. What sort of job would allow for all that? Neither of them has a degree or any sort of work experience beyond painting and gardening. Maybe it's a large house that needs to be completely reworked. Shuvai could have sold himself as the building manager, needing to hire a team of workers, knowing full well that it would only be the two of them working harder than five lazy men could.

Whatever it is, it could change their lives completely.

Their house might have a spare room. It could be a painting room, full of an assortment of colors waiting for him. Or maybe this new venture will require them to have a study, filled with important paperwork and phone calls. They could have an answering machine and his sisters could leave messages for him.

They could entertain. People could come over for dinners. He could make Flora some tea and toast for a change. Toast! If they could afford to rent an entire house, then surely they will be able to buy a toaster? No more heating stale bread on the two-plate.

They could get a good second-hand oven; he would be able to fix it up. It would smell of food before any cooking began. Who would he invite over? Besides Shuvai, he doesn't have any real friends.

He would start to make some. Surely people with houses aren't lonely? Flora would love his place. He could even bring his younger sister over from Zimbabwe. His eyes shine.

"So, are you coming? He said we mustn't be late." Shuvai is standing at their excuse for a door that only slightly dampens the fantasy. Runyararo's feet purposefully step outside of the rusted present. Their ill-equipped clothes are no match for the callous Joburg winter. But today it feels like life is percolating.

Runyararo thinks that he finally understands what it means to be the bee's knees because even his knees are bouncing in excitement and he has never been one for dancing. The smell of urine avoids their noses, respecting the newly-found status of their walk.

Their strides lengthen as they move toward Yeoville, Dunbar Street. They slow down, scanning the houses, not noticing the cracked walls or the untended gardens struggling to maintain grass.

All of the houses are ground level. Number 68 is full of potential. The peeling peach wall sits neatly under Runyararo's chin. It has two black gates, one for cars and a smaller one with a latch for people. He stares into the yard. A stone walkway leads toward a polished stoep and a wooden door; three burglar-barred windows stare out at the street. The house has an extra eye. The oddity is warming.

Runyararo can see a midnight blue wall and a bright yellow house, with purple flowers along the side, perhaps eventually a car in the driveway. Neither of them has their license so maybe some bicycles until then. It's perfect, no stairs, no neighbors right up against you and no terrifying views into the night's mayhem.

No stairs. His mother could visit him in a place like this.

"Hai, hai, hai! Nothing to look at here! You want me to call the police?" A squealing voice from a large woman dressed in neon orange and resembling the Oros man, waddling out from the back door, speeds their journey up again.

Shuvai is laughing uncontrollably but Runyararo can't stop thinking about what it would be like to have two entrances and a garden.

They pass a group of children buying cigarettes from an old man. The old man sitting at his stall, with a few odd pieces of fruit, sweets and loose cigarettes, is pleased to see his regulars and passes the children a box of matches.

Runyararo never had the courage to do anything like that as a child; he was too scared of getting caught and too certain of the rules.

Rules have never done him much good.

## 11

# CATHLEEN
*It's all stuck*

She's in a room stacked with cardboard boxes. It smells like flour and mothballs. Her head is heavy. She can barely lift it in order to look around.

"Hello?" Her voice is thin and dry. It disappears into the boxes, abandoning her in the silence. A low humming vibrates under the floor. Like the noise of a fridge that can only be heard when there is no competing noise. She clears her throat. She needs something to drink.

She has to force her knees to bend; there are cuts on her legs that sting as they brush across the dusty floor. She kicks her heels off and pulls herself up, balancing her weight on the boxes. One box under her right hand starts to slip and she sees it all happen in slow motion. It's still too fast for her to react. Her hand fumbles past the box as it crashes and cocoon-like white balls roll across the floor.

Her knees buckle.

"Hey!" A pointy-toed shoe taps at her shoulder, revealing a diamond-printed maroon sock covering an ankle just below the sharp fold of hemmed black trousers. It's the man with the red tie.

His eyes are a pale blue and perfectly framed by thick dark lashes. He looks like sunshine, badly dressed but a ray of magnificence nonetheless. Her hand climbs up his leg as she tries to pull herself back up. He steps back and she falls forward. He rolls her over onto her back with the tip of his shoe.

Her head is aching. She needs a cigarette.

"You ready to behave yet?" His accent is a strange mixture of Afrikaans and American. He looks like a smoker. Maybe he has one for her.

Her lips crack as she parts them but no words come. Instead a thin trickle of warm blood starts to navigate its way to her chin.

What should she say? She hasn't done anything wrong. She nods her head slowly.

"Someone's here to see you." Eddie stands in the doorway. He doesn't look at her.

"I'm coming." Lionel nods at Eddie. "I'll be back for that information soon, sweetheart."

The door closes.

When James was little, she would slam her bedroom door closed, keeping him out of her room. He would wait for her to come out. Always smiling and wanting to tell her about his stupid day. Her mother would scream at her to open her door for James and let him inside. But he seemed content to wait. She stopped being his idol in recent years. When their mother died, he was very brave, acting like the older sibling. They slept in his bed that night. She cried into his shoulder until she fell asleep. If only he were here now, maybe she'd be able to fall asleep.

# 12

# RUNYARARO
*Nothing can escape*

They turn into Innes Street and stare up toward the large hill they must still climb. The road is bumpy. On the opposite side, he sees a woman sitting at a bus stop. She looks out of place. Her crisp white dress and red jersey shine bright against the rusted metal bench, like a Valentine's card placed on an empty shelf.

They cross the road.

What would he say to an elegant woman like her? His hands fidget, straightening out his clothing, until he shoves them into his pockets.

She lifts her head and looks at him. He can't believe it. It's Flora.

She quickly grabs the plastic bag next to her and gasps as she sees Runyararo.

Does she believe that he's a thief? He didn't stand up for himself. He was stupid to think that she would think otherwise.

"Hello, sweetness." This is what Shuvai says to all women whose names he can't remember. Flora is clutching the plastic bag tightly. It looks like there are shoes inside it. Her skin seems paler than Runyararo remembers and now it looks like she might cry. "Been a while, hasn't it?"

Flora ignores Shuvai and stares at Runyararo.

Shuvai isn't used to his big flashy smile not having the desired effect. "Well, it was good to see you. We have to run, got a big job lined up. I'll call you sometime. Maybe we can go out once I start earning the big bucks," he laughs, as he starts walking away.

Flora hasn't stopped staring at Runyararo. It momentarily glues him to the pavement.

"You can't call me if you don't have my number." Her voice struggles to come out of her mouth as her eyes remain transfixed.

Shuvai turns around and asks for her number. He doesn't take it down when she says it.

Runyararo closes his eyes and imagines each number. He remembers them by assigning a color and an object to each numeral—something that began when he first started school. Now it's second nature. Zero is a black ball, seven an orange umbrella, three a blue bee, six a green mop, five a pink chair, nine a brown lamp, four a gray ladder, two a white bus, eight a red snake and one a yellow wall. The ball rolls under the umbrella squashing the bee, which needs to be mopped, lift the chair and push it behind the lamp, get the ladder and climb the two-story bus, slide down the snake and rest against the wall. He repeats the story in his head.

Not even the large houses in Observatory distract him.

He turns around abruptly and follows Shuvai's footsteps until they get to Kensington.

What was Flora doing there? There were so many things he wanted to say to her.

"This is it man." They're standing outside a semi-detached house. What are they doing here? This one, No. 12A, has a large gate and the top of the wall has pieces of broken glass stuck to it. The afternoon sunlight hits the multi-colored glass and gives it a religious feeling. Next door 12B is more homely. There is a black toy motorbike in the garden and a welcome mat outside the door; the occupants there seem significantly less concerned about safety than those at 12A.

Shuvai rings the bell. "Be cool man, just follow my lead." He shifts from one foot to the other as though he is trying to kill ants. Runyararo is uneasy.

"Yes?" The voice coming from the intercom is abrupt.

"Uh ja, we are here...to see Mister...uh...Lionel. He told us to come by today."

The buzzer is short. It feels as rude as the voice from the intercom. Shuvai looks like he is holding his breath as he pushes the gate open, walks in and closes it behind them.

The yard is small and almost completely cemented. The only signs of green are the weeds that push through the cracks in the cement. The men step tentatively toward the door, unable to look at each other. Shuvai shakes his arm before making a fist to knock on the solid wooden door. None of this reflects the promising future that Shuvai spoke so eagerly about.

As his dry knuckles are about to knock for the second time, the door swings open.

A woman with a missing tooth and high-waisted trousers opens the door. She is dirty. Her hair is matted. She doesn't say anything but turns and leads them into a room that looks like an office. Runyararo sees white dust on her black top, like a Milky Way of dandruff.

There is a large table with a single chair behind it. They are left alone in the room. The walls are completely bare and the beige carpet is spotted with brown stains. Runyararo finally turns to look at Shuvai. What has he got them into now? How will these filthy people be able to pay them enough to rent a whole house?

The door closes behind them. A man in a suit and a red tie walks past them and takes the only seat in the room. "Welcome, gentlemen." He doesn't sound South African.

"Uh...hello Mr. Lionel."

"Good to meet you." He stretches out his hand to shake theirs. They have to lean over the table to do so. "We're tremendously happy to have you both on board." His hand feels soft against Runyararo's calloused one. Maybe this won't be as bad as Runyararo thought. This man is groomed and charming. "Did you find the place alright?"

"Yes, sir. No troubles." Shuvai is calming down and rests against the table.

"You want anything to drink? Tea? Coffee?"

"No thanks. We are fine. Thanks, sir."

Has Shuvai completely lost his manners? You must always accept an offer of a drink. Runyararo's mother would kill him if she heard that he was rude to someone's politeness.

"Excellent. I can tell that you two have your wits about you."

He smiles warmly as he rests back into his chair. "Right. Well I suppose on to the business then. Shuvai, as we discussed, you two will be doing basic deliveries. The woman you met earlier will always be here to help you. If there are any problems, please don't hesitate to ask her for help. Her name is Dina. I would like to be of more assistance but unfortunately I'm not around all that often."

"Thank you, Mr. Lionel. I'm sure we won't have any problems."

"One other thing gentlemen, this business is a sensitive one." He leans forward. "So it's probably best that you don't use my name. And not a word to anyone about what you do or hear. You will receive R1200 each at the end of every week. It will be on this table, in a brown envelope, every Friday. Any special jobs will mean an extra thousand for each of you. Are we happy?"

"Yes, Mr. Lionel." They should leave.

"I told you. Forget that name." His eyes go dark.

"Sorry...uh...sir." Shuvai backs away from the table. This isn't the kind of man that you can walk away from.

"Can you drive?"

"Yes, but...no license."

"Not a problem, not a problem." His eyes turn to Runyararo: "And you? Do you understand English?" Runyararo is stuck.

"He can't talk Mister...since he was a child, not a word."

"Can't talk, hey?" He smiles and looks Runyararo up and down.

"Great stuff." He laughs to himself. "For today, gentlemen, the job is simple: there are some boxes in the room on the right. Take the ones marked with blue crosses to this address." He hands Runyararo a piece of paper. "Delivery needs to be by seven sharp, now get going."

They are still for the longest minutes.

The man keeps his eyes focused on the table. Shuvai finally opens the door and exhales. Runyararo keeps as close to him as possible.

"Hey, Mr. Silent." Runyararo turns back. Lionel tosses him a set of keys. "Take the white Golf. Get moving now." They hurry out of the room and away from the potential storm of a man.

The door on the right opens into what seems like a storage space the size of a small bedroom. There are cardboard boxes everywhere. Each of the boxes has a different colored marking on it: red ticks, yellow lines, orange dots and blue crosses.

"And now? Where do you think you are?" It's the woman who let them in. She pushes past them. "This is not your house. You wait by the door."

Shuvai knocks a box over with his knee in his rush to get out. It remains closed.

"Fuck, man! Watch yourself." She brings the boxes out one at a time. Shuvai takes the first three to the car. They are not particularly heavy, lighter than a 5-liter tin of paint but she struggles to move the single one that she carries.

Runyararo watches her become increasingly slower as she coughs her way between the boxes and the doorway. It's a thick cough, rattling with fluids.

Shuvai is back by the time the next three are out. Runyararo grabs them and rushes away from the exhausted woman. She must have some sort of disease. He puts them down next to the car. There is a thick film of dirt on the handle of the boot. It only has enough room to fit the first six boxes. He leans back against the grime and closes his eyes in the winter sun.

The last time he saw his mother, she and the rest of his family were walking him out. The goodbyes took forever. She eventually sat down in the dirt, something he had never seen her do before. Her wide red skirt made a perfect semicircle in front of her. Her eyes squinted up at him as he walked toward her and eventually provided shade from the glaring sun. There was such relief in her face, some of her wrinkles disappeared. She was sad but proud of him for leaving and standing on his own as a man.

She must be so old now.

Shuvai stumbles outside with four boxes hindering his vision.

Runyararo heads back inside. Shuvai should have found out more before getting them into this mess. He must have known that this was not an ordinary job. All he could think of was the money. And it didn't sound like enough to warrant this kind of work. It was stupid of Shuvai to think that this would be their way out.

After a long and laborious process fifteen boxes have made their way to the car. The men arrange and rearrange them, trying to get them all in. The cardboard puzzle eventually fits together awkwardly with odd angles and no solid borderline. One box remains outside. Shuvai grabs it and sits with it on his lap in the passenger seat, blending into the scene behind him.

How can he decide to be the passenger? This whole thing was his idea.

Runyararo shouldn't be shocked. This is what Shuvai has been doing from the start. Finding work for him to do and then claiming a percentage of the pay, without doing anything himself. The surprise is that Shuvai carried any boxes at all. Now, he sits there like the King's uncle, staring out of the window, waiting to be chauffeur driven to see the sights.

Runyararo's body swells from anger. He's ready to sort Shuvai out, once and for all, and he won't need a voice to make his point.

"Hey man, go back in and have a look around. Make sure there aren't any other blue crosses." Shuvai is speaking so fast the words don't make sense. Runyararo whips open the passenger door and tears at Shuvai's thin cotton shirt. He brings his face down close to Shuvai's. Sweat races down his face dripping onto Shuvai. It's as salty as tears. Shuvai tries to look away but his head is secured by Runyararo's left hand, firmly clenching Shuvai's jaw.

What now? Runyararo lets go and storms back toward the house.

Dina isn't there anymore. Runyararo opens the door to the store-room and scans the boxes as best as he can from the doorway.

They have to find a way to get out of this job.

There is an assortment of colors: black half-moons, orange dots, purple squares, and then he sees a leg. A white person's leg, pale and unmoving, peeps from behind the boxes with purple squares. It's a smooth leg and the person it belongs to isn't wearing any shoes. Dina was definitely wearing shoes and trousers.

The passage is quiet. He enters the room and moves closer to see that it's a girl lying face down on the floor. Her skirt has risen up around her waist. Maybe he should cover her. He looks around but can't see anything.

What if she's dead? If they find him here, he could be next. But he can't just leave. He kneels down and she moves, ever so slightly. He is back up and heading for the door. What kind of people are they working for? This is starting to look like a quick ride to jail and then back over the border. What would his family say?

He is out the front door and inserts the key into the ignition.

His feet are trembling. Why was that woman in the room? He stalls the car repeatedly for at least five minutes. The revving brings Dina to his window.

"Can't you drive?" He shakes his head as if to say no but he means to say yes. He has driven before but his foot won't obey his mind.

"He has. Just getting used to the car. We'll be fine." If Shuvai is so assured, why doesn't he drive?

"Okay, go easy on the clutch there. Any damages to the car and it'll come out of your pay. Now stop messing around and get out of here."

Runyararo slowly starts the car again, puts it into gear, looks in his rear-view mirror and gives it some petrol.

The car jerks forward. Dina gives him another dirty look.

He puts the gear into reverse now and finally moves backwards out of the driveway.

Getting out onto the road doesn't make him feel any better. This car must be stolen. Why would Lionel allow two men without licenses to take his car out? The cops would have a field day with them, two Zimbabweans without license, in a stolen car, carrying drugs or guns or whatever illegal thing is in those boxes. What if they're being set up to distract from something else Lionel is doing?

After knocking two curbs, stalling at three traffic lights and getting properly lost, they arrive at a complex in Hyde Park a few minutes after eight. Runyararo shows Shuvai the piece of paper and takes note of all the security cameras in this complex. He doesn't know which way to go.

The guard wants to know what number they're going to.

"Number 2." Runyararo sees a white bus.

"What is your name?" The guard approaches them with a visitor's registration book.

Silence.

"Blue Cross." How did Shuvai know to say that? Has he done this sort of thing before? Is this what he's been doing while Runyararo has been busy painting homes?

"Hello, sir. Blue Cross is here for you."

The gate opens. They enter and Runyararo struggles to park in the single bay outside number 2.

"You're late." A man with a long face shows them where to take the boxes.

# 13

# FARHANA
*Folds within folds*

"The house is looking awesome. The painting has come a long way." Her eye enjoys the coated look but the smell of lingering paint stretches inside her and flips her stomach like a pancake.

"Ja...my mom had to fire the painter. The asshole was stealing. You can't trust these people." Zee opens the door and lets her in.

"We going to your room or do you want to watch TV?"

Farhana's eyes take the room in. It's still incredible to her. The walls all have real paintings on them, with signatures at the bottom and everything, not just gold-plated gaudy mosque pictures and prayers everywhere. She can't understand most of the artwork and probably wouldn't think of buying any of it but is impressed with how classy and expensive it all looks.

An oil painting at the base of the stairs grabs her attention. It is a portrait of a woman with a mound of hair that blurs into the mountains in the background. The woman's features are blurred. To Farhana it looks like the artist got bored midway and left the painting incomplete. There are no eyes in the painting and she wonders whether it would be accepted into a Muslim home, where eyes are never displayed.

As she turns to Zee, a pencil sketch of four prowling hyenas, placed a centimeter or two above his head, screams out at her. The hyenas are all moving forward as though they are about to step out of the canvas, their heads slightly tilted as they stare at her.

"Upstairs. I want to show you something on the computer."

She follows him up the stairs avoiding the stares of the hyenas. She notices that the door to the master bedroom is open. The king-sized bed is unmade and a pair of holey socks is lying on the floor next to some trousers. Zee's parents are divorced. He keeps telling her about the luxury of getting money from both sides. Does his mother just bring men home? A man's brown work shoe lies in the doorway. The sole is worn and has started to fray at the edges like it has suffered an unbearable weight.

There is a photograph on the bedside table. It is of a white woman holding a baby in her arms. The frame is a solid whitewashed wooden structure that houses the woman delicately. She has soft blonde curls cut into a bob that ends just above her jawline and her gaze is powerful and direct.

"Zee, who is that in the photo?"

"Hey? What photo?"

"On your mother's bedside table."

"It's...don't look in there! It's the maid's day off. She's not here for one day and the whole place gets a little crazy." He leans in and pulls the door closed. "It must be a new frame. It's just the picture that it comes with. I'm sure my mom will put a killer one of me in there soon."

Zee's room is a total mess. Farhana can't imagine her room ever looking like this, never mind going out while it's in such a state. She makes her bed every morning and tidies the few things that are out of place. Her mother would kill her if she didn't. "Who do you think is going to clean this up? Huh?" she would say. But then again, her mother would never leave her own bedroom looking like Zee's mother's room. Farhana doesn't have a maid but she's sure that even if they did, this would not be acceptable.

They go into Zee's room. She struggles to find uncovered carpet to walk on so as not to step on any of his clothes. She doesn't recognize any of them. But then again Zee is always buying new clothes. A pair of gray pants that look way too small, even for Zee's scrawny body, are crumpled on the bed.

"Like I said...maid's day off." He tosses the pants to the side and his mouth gives way to his uncertain smile. It's the smile that made her want to show off her dimples.

They met at a house party in Greenside. She wasn't invited. Her friend Jeena had been asked to go by a guy that she was interested in and she begged Farhana to go with her so she didn't have to drive the whole way alone. Jeena ditched her as soon as they arrived. It was not the type of crowd that Farhana was used to. There were no Indians; well, there were a couple but they dressed and spoke like the white people.

Farhana stood back and watched the crowd, looking for hints of how to socialize with this hipster bunch. Zee was easy to observe and seemed to know everyone there.

Every so often, he glanced at her. She was the new face standing against the wall. She kept biting through her polystyrene cup and held the orange-slice shaped pieces in her hand. Her body and eyes refused to be still. It was a swing between attempting to look comfortable and wanting to disappear completely.

Her sequined top was a clear indicator that she was an outsider. The rest of the crowd wore old-looking mismatched clothes, many in thick-rimmed glasses, with heavy fringes, and two of the guys had long thick beards that could rival her uncle's.

Zee watched her squirm as he made his rounds—acting like the party was being thrown for him. He made sure that all the other guests felt appropriately acknowledged.

She was jealous of his ease. He would raise his skinny arm and casually play with his short dreadlocks. Then he would wipe the back of his hand across his broad forehead, tilt his chin up and let out a broken laugh. It was unnatural and forced. He was a fake, playing the game better than most of the others but it was still dishonest.

She wanted to leave the party but Jeena was nowhere to be seen, when Zee came her way. He stared straight at her. It was uncomfortable. She wriggled like a worm and didn't feel attractive at all but later he said he had thought it was cute.

Her face was unfamiliar and full like the moon. His cheeks lifted toward his eyes, making space for his teeth to bare themselves in something between a question and a smile. He seemed different with her. She felt that this smile was real and honest in its oddness. She smiled back at him with a dimple in each cheek. He said he liked them, they made her balanced.

That question mark of a smile annoys her now. She has seen it so often that she knows it has nothing to do with honesty. It is his easy-way-out smile. It works on everyone in any situation. And here he is using it on her, again. She smiles half-heartedly with one side of her mouth, offering him a single dimple. He moves to the computer so fast, she doesn't know if he even noticed. He doesn't seem to notice much when it comes to her anymore. His back is facing her and he is already tapping away at the keyboard.

Why won't he just sit and talk to her? She wants to be held. She wants him to make her feel safe. If only he would take her hand and talk to her like the first time she sat on this bed, she wouldn't feel like she was disappearing. As soon as he started talking to her, she relaxed. He had made her feel special.

She had struggled to find the right things to say. He was so cool and promised to take her to all the hotspots in Joburg. She had lied many times in that conversation, claiming to have been to more than half of the places he mentioned, when mostly she was either at home or at

The Zone in Rosebank watching movies or walking around with friends. The worst thing she had ever done before meeting Zee was sharing a cigarette with a friend and then it was more about the fun of covering it up with gum and deodorant than the actual smoking.

She wanted him to find her exciting. She still wants that.

"Damn! The internet is messing up. You want a drink?" He clicks his fingers like he's trying to remember something. "Think I saw some wine in a cabinet downstairs." He's back on his feet.

"No. It's...I'm...I shouldn't."

"Why not, babes?"

"I...well, I haven't eaten today."

"Naughty girl. You know I don't like coat hangers. I'll make you something. You want a sandwich? Ham and cheese?" He's already at the door. How many times does she have to tell him that she doesn't eat pork?

"No. I'm fasting Zee."

"Really? Hectic. Okay. Well, why don't we watch TV then?"

He is pacing the room. He keeps moving between the door and the computer, completely unconcerned about the clothes he keeps walking over. Is he thinking about breaking up with her? Is she boring him? Why can't he relax?

"Zee. Please come and sit down with me. Let's talk."

"Everything okay?"

He sits down on the bed next to her and attempts to look compassionate but his pupils are the size of five rand coins. He's high. She's been so consumed by her own stuff that she hadn't noticed until now. There's no point in trying to talk to him when he's like this.

"Everything is fine. I'm just tired, that's all. Let's go see what movies are on TV."

He's back at the door in a flash. "Going to the toilet, meet you downstairs."

She makes her way down. There's nothing worse than being with Zee when he's high. He keeps promising that he'll stop but his promises are meaning less and less these days.

"You want some water?" Zee skips down the stairs two at a time.

"No thanks, not allowed while I'm fasting."

"Oh snap! Well, you don't mind if I have some, do you?"

Cocaine also means that he doesn't care about anyone but himself.

"It's fine, Zee! Do whatever the fuck you want!" A voice snaps from inside her. It shocks her and, from the look on his face, he seems pretty surprised by it too. She doesn't usually raise her voice; her anger is generally cold and filled with silences.

"I'm sorry, baby. I'm being insensitive, I know. Let's just watch a movie. How about I give you a back rub?"

There's that smile again. She takes a cushion and sits on the floor in front of the couch.

He jumps up and races to the kitchen. When he walks back in, he's gulping down a glass of water. He sits behind her, sandwiching her between his legs.

There is something wrong with the DSTV. A red light flashes on the machine. He presses the menu button and opens the message. He has to close one eye to read that the connection has been suspended until the account is paid. "Fuck!" He throws the remote on the floor and stands up so fast he stumbles and falls over her, accidently kicking her in the stomach. He rolls on the floor laughing. He sounds like a hyena.

"Come on, Zee, that was fucking sore." She's holding herself.

He crawls back toward her. "I'm sorry baby, let me make it better." He starts kissing her stomach. Then he moves to her neck and continues up toward her mouth. At first it's gentle and reluctantly she starts softening into him.

He pulls back and stares at her. "Show me my dimples." She smiles and places her mouth on his. Her hands slip under his shirt and rub his back. His skin is slightly damp from the drugs but she's enjoying the tenderness.

His fingers struggle with the buttons on her shirt but she doesn't help him. She's happy not to rush and wants to keep kissing. She's feeling bloated and she'd rather not have him see that so she rolls on top of him, trapping his hands between their bodies.

He extracts them and strokes her hair. "You're spectacular."

"Zilindile!" A woman in white is standing behind the couch.

Zee is miraculously on his feet as Farhana struggles to get up.

"Ma."

"What are you doing here?" The woman's mouth is agape. There's enough space to rest a golf ball in it. She is clutching a plastic bag to her chest.

"Ma, can we please talk outside?" He steps forward. Farhana doesn't know if she should speak or not.

"Hi mam. I'm Farhana."

Zee shoots her a look, confirming that silence is a better option.

His mother doesn't even bother to look at her.

"What if Mr. Joseph came home? Hai, Zilindile, this is too much!"

Is Mr. Joseph the man whose things are in the master bedroom?

"I'll wait outside." Farhana moves toward the front door.

"Hey! Out the back door. You want to behave like a cockroach, you leave like one."

"Sorry, mam."

Standing in the garden Farhana sees the maid's room at the back. It looks only slightly larger than her bedroom. Looking down at her shirt, three buttons over her belly are undone. Her tears travel down her face and fall onto her exposed stomach.

Zee's mother steps outside. She looks at Farhana and clicks her tongue, shaking her head, before walking to the maid's room.

There have been too many lies.

"Look, Farhana, my mum is mad angry. You better go. I'll call you later."

"How am I going to go, Zee? I didn't miraculously get a car or anything."

He reaches into his pocket and pulls out a twenty rand note.

"Here. Sorry, but I have to deal with this." He follows his mother to the back room.

She makes her way round the side of the house and lets herself out. She starts walking down the street. It all starts to sink in. She re-buttons her shirt but she can't stop crying. The sounds that are coming from her are loud for this quiet neighborhood. The street is empty and eventually she stops and leans against one of the large jacaranda trees and tries to think of a plan. She has never taken a taxi before. Which of those signs is supposed to take you home?

Everything was a lie. What is she going to do? Who will be able to fetch her now? Anyone leaving from Lenz would take an hour to get here and then there would still be the traffic getting back. By then it will be long after they break fast. Her mother is going to be furious.

She continues to walk, turning randomly until she sees a street lined with restaurants.

She sits down at the emptiest one and checks the menu to see what twenty rand will get her.

"Just a coffee please. Decaf with hot milk."

The restaurant is minimally decorated and very white.

Everything is white: the tiles, the tablecloths, the chairs. It's sterile. She laughs. The only thing that's black are the waiters.

Her coffee arrives. She likes it creamy.

A woman in purple snakeskin heels with a matching handbag and a baby in a pram walks into the restaurant and sits at the table behind Farhana. The baby starts to cry. The sound is shaky, like a lamb.

Farhana turns around and sees manicured hands slide into the pram and pick up the smallest bundle of a human being imaginable. How is this woman so thin after having a baby?

The woman brings the baby up to her shoulder, shaking the little bundle and shushing it. The baby doesn't stop. She sniffs its nappy; her eyes start to look agitated.

She notices Farhana staring at her and starts to frantically search the pram until she pulls out a bottle. The baby gives it a few sucks and starts to calm down.

The woman stands with her baby, rocking back and forth in her beautiful shoes. How does she manage to do that while still looking glamorous?

Farhana smiles. The woman is singing softly to her child. She recognizes the melody. It's something her father used to hum when he worked around the house.

She turns back to her coffee. It's cold now.

# 14

# FRANK
*Falling over can be grounding*

The house is muted. Cathleen is disappearing; he can't remember the last time he saw her. Tonight James is sleeping at a friend's and Flora has taken Zilindile to her mother.

Old houses are never completely quiet. The darker it gets, the more the structure complains about its age. He's got the TV on to keep him company but it's not helping much with only the SABC and e.tv working.

This was the moment. It was what he and Jennifer dreamed about—the ultimate freedom from endless noise and the administration of other people's lives. There are no responsibilities tonight, no one to drop off or pick up, no lunches or dinners to make, just a night off.

There's nothing to celebrate without her. He knows that it's the start of many nights like this to follow.

He misses the kids. He's angry with Jennifer for not being around for this. She kept things operational. She was the fun one, the one who made the plans, the spontaneous one who could just as easily break the schedules, the one who looked after him and the kids. She fought with him about not getting involved enough but he thought she enjoyed being in control of it all. She had everything on her shoulders.

Tonight he will do what they always planned. He will make it up to her. He changes the channel and finds some music on SABC1, which he doesn't recognize at all. It's a strangely repetitive song about cell-phones and Facebook. Technology baffles him. He doesn't even know what half the functions on his phone are meant to do. These social networking things terrify him. Why would anyone put all their personal details onto the internet? Then to share that information with complete strangers and chat to people you've never actually met, it seems ludicrous.

There is no sense of real connection anymore. A friend of his has been trying to get him to set up an online dating profile. He's not ready to move on yet but even if he was, why would he start with someone he has never seen? What would he even write about himself? "A middle-age widower with two children, no job, who is getting fatter by the minute, is looking for...What?" It's just ridiculous. When he's ready, he'll go out and meet someone the normal way. He's not like the kids or even Flora who are always on their phones. Sometimes they get so sucked in they don't even realize he's talking to them.

People who live at the coast must speak more. The outdoors surely helps with that? Moving away from Johannesburg will be great for him and the kids. It would be like the holidays. Jennifer planned the greatest trips. The four of them away from school and work was always magical. It's a chance to hit the reset button.

He goes over to the CD rack in the corner. He wipes away a thick film of dust with the palm of his hand, which he then wipes on his chinos. He must speak to Flora about cleaning the forgotten areas.

Amongst the mixture of old folk, classical, rock and the few soul albums is *Cold Fact* by Rodriguez. It's not really something he would have chosen to play and he hasn't heard it in years.

"Sugar Man" fills the room. It brings him back to Jennifer when they were both still young and romantic. She introduced him to Rodriguez. He wasn't very hip.

She introduced him to a world of new music and loved to study his face as he listened for the first time. She wanted him to be honest with her about how the music made him feel. To him it was just music. Sometimes there was an enjoyable melody but he never felt the eye-opening heart-rending shift that she wanted to hear about.

The first time she played this album was when they still lived in a tiny garden cottage on the edge of someone's property. She had a joint with her. He had never smoked dope and was terrified that the landlord would smell something but he was so in love with her, he would have done anything.

He coughed through an entire song. She was sweet enough not to laugh. There was nothing enjoyable about it. The words that came out of his mouth sounded foreign.

Later that night he made love to her. He had wanted to take her to the bedroom but she insisted on staying in the lounge. The tiled floor made their bodies cold and he bruised both his knees.

Jennifer claimed that Cathleen was conceived that night.

According to his calculations that would have been impossible but he didn't argue. Jennifer was secretly such a romantic.

A little Jameson from his secret liquor stash behind the encyclopedias on the bookcase helps him to relax. His burly shoulders slowly sink into a relaxed position. He raises the bottle as a toast to Jennifer through the music. He peels off his shoes with his feet, exposing holey socks and gives his weight to the last soldiering springs in the couch as he gulps from the bottle.

It's only the first sip that's harsh.

He sings along with the music, not trying to sound like Rodriguez but rather like Jennifer. She had a terrible voice. His pitch-perfect ear won't allow him to spoil the song in the same way. He laughs.

After a while the whiskey has done its trick. He lifts his large body onto his feet. Why isn't she here? She was definitely the better dancer. He starts to sway and then his hands are clapping along. One more swig and his body is contorting every which way to the slow and steady beat.

"I wonder how many times you've been had." His tongue stretches the words out of sync but his well-tuned voice blends acceptably with Rodriguez. It's his favorite song on the album.

When he heard it, all he could think was that he had only been had by her and he was happy to leave it at that. He could've been a singer. Jennifer always said that. They used to love karaoke. Well, he loved it. He stomps around the carpet and allows his head to swing along with the rhythm. This was their dream, to get drunk—well Jennifer thought that a little joint wouldn't hurt—and turn the lounge into their very own karaoke spot. Then they were going to make love and fall asleep right there.

The windows of the lounge reflect the old dancing bear. He sees himself and stops moving. The sight is too much to handle. The house is lonely. This is silly. Without her this can't be normal. He was stupid to even put this CD on. He stops the music and wipes his face. The silence is hollow.

He sits back down and searches the channels. His mind can't focus on anything. He turns the TV off.

A red light flashes on his Blackberry. There's an email from the estate agent. She's been nagging him since the evaluation of the house. He thought he was ready but he's not. They need to move.

He can't sustain this house but he's not ready to leave Jennifer. She chose this house. She decorated it. Her smell sometimes finds him when he least expects it.

He's heard about a job opening in Cape Town. He hasn't responded. He needs the money but what if things change too much? What if he never smells her again? Jennifer would have been able to handle this. She should be the one living.

He turns his phone off.

What now? The silence is suffocating. The whiskey is finished. He goes to his secret stash but there's only some peppermint liqueur. He can't just sit here.

He grabs his car keys and goes outside. The outside light bulbs need to be replaced. He staggers toward the garage door and fumbles around the spider webs until he finds the latch and pulls it open. It's louder than expected, announcing his presence to the empty street. Rushing in from the cold and back to the car, he speeds out, knocking the left brake light against the side of the gate. "Fuck!" He pauses and looks up and down the street and then back at the gate. He should close it but he just wants to get away. He drives off.

As soon as he gets to the stop street, the petrol light comes on. He makes his way to Parkhurst, which isn't too far away.

There aren't any available parking spaces on the main road and he doesn't feel up to parallel parking, so he drives a block down one of the side streets before finding an easy enough parking space. Two one hundred rand notes are stashed in the cubbyhole and should be enough to take care of his night. He stumbles out of the car and straight into a car guard.

"Sorry, sir." Where did this guy appear from? He swears they're getting sneakier by the minute. He stares at the guard, who seems unsure of what to do in response. Frank stumbles backwards slightly and then swerves around the guard to make his way up to the main road. "I will watch it nicely, sir," the man calls after him and Frank waves his arm in a suggestion that he's heard it.

He doesn't go out alone. It's not the way things are supposed to be. The bars look happy, badly lit and consumed with people. The restaurants seem worse; they have romantic lighting and atmospheric music. His whiskey courage is fast depleting as he gets closer to the main strip. Which place will be the most accommodating?

He doesn't want to sit out on the pavement. That was Jennifer's style, not his. She loved watching people and being watched. He could barely handle it when she was with him. Now he wants to hide. But as he walks, each place looks worse than the previous one. The crowd is younger than he remembers. A middle-aged man walks past him with solid determination. He decides to follow the man into a small enclosed bar.

The crowd is mixed. The men range from young twenty-somethings to a few geezers who look older than Frank but all the women are very young. There are no free stools at the bar. He orders a beer and stands awkwardly in a corner near the toilets. The smell of urine is potent and blends into the thickness of the heavily breathing bodies. It feels lonelier than being at home. A group of young women are sitting at a table near him. They are loud and giggly. What is he doing here? Perhaps he can buy some beers to take home. The bartender is too busy to listen to his whispered concerns, so Frank just orders another beer and retreats to his position.

A young girl walks toward him. Her legs are long for her body, like an awkward blue crane but she is incredibly thin. He could fold her up and insert her into the cumbersome handbag weighing down her arm.

"Hi, Mr. Joseph." Her eyes look up at him. She smells sweet, like cheap perfume.

"Hello?" The alcohol makes it impossible for him to hide his confusion.

"It's me, Lucy." He has no clue who she is. "I was at school with Cathleen." Her lips are pert and turn down slightly at the sides like she has just eaten something sour.

He scans the room for Cathleen. His height gives him quite an advantage but he doesn't see his child.

"Oh." He still doesn't remember this girl.

"How is Cathleen? She's at Wits right?" He doesn't want to speak to this overly confident kid.

"Uh...yes. She's fine, good. Taking a year off, after...She needed a break." He takes a big gulp of his beer. Some of it slips out of his mouth and runs down his chin onto his shirt. He starts to wipe it off with his hand. Why doesn't she just leave him alone?

"Here you go." She holds out a tissue. He takes it from her and dabs his shirt.

"Thanks, good to see you. I'll tell Cathleen I saw you."

"Actually, Mr. Joseph, could I ask you a favor?" She leans in toward him. The sweetness of her perfume starts to overwhelm him but he can't move back.

"Uh, okay. Yes. What is it?"

"I've forgotten my wallet at home. Do you think you could buy me a drink?"

These kids are all the same. "What do you want?"

"A double vodka and a Red Bull." She smiles at him with her perfect teeth.

They head to the bar together. It's more crowded now but people part to accommodate his mass. She leans into him, fitting snugly under his armpit. Her drink costs him seventy-three rand. How is that possible? He hands her the drink, expecting her to disappear into the crowd. "And two tequilas, please," she pipes up. The bartender nods, a small smile creeping onto his face. What must he be thinking?

Frank looks around. All these faces are seeing him. They're seeing him with this child tucked under his arm and he feels them becoming increasingly judgmental. He wants to tell them that she's just his daughter's friend. Would that make it worse? The bartender hands him the new bill. One hundred and three rand! He tries to look into his pocket without her noticing. There's just enough for one more beer. He hands over his cash. He miscalculated and is seven rand short but they have the drinks and the beer is open.

He reluctantly fishes out his over-used credit card.

"Can I add a ten percent tip?" The bartender's smile is now in full bloom. What a smug bastard.

"Sure."

"No, no wait. Leave the tab open for now." Her little voice creeps out from under his arm. She seems intent on bankrupting him tonight. Don't her parents give her money? It's irresponsible not to give a girl like this enough cash. She could very easily end up asking the wrong kind of guy for drinks. He can't say no.

They down their tequilas. Her entire body shakes and he notices the firmness of her little breasts. He feels perverted.

"Do you want to sit down? My friends have a table over there."

There are three other girls about her age and a man slightly younger than Frank. He's glad not to see Cathleen. He nods and gets another beer before steering the way to the table. The girls shift over to make space for him on the stained cushioned seat and continue with their conversation. He leaves no room for her to sit but his head is spinning too fast for him to stand. She doesn't look bothered and sits down on his lap. Her bum is bony and pierces into his thigh. Cathleen used to sit on his knee all the time.

He should leave.

"Please can I borrow your phone for a second?" Her hand is so close to his crotch he can feel the heat of it.

"Left it at home." He should have read that email. He should go home. Another sip of beer enters his mouth. She turns toward her friends, treating him like he's a seat. It feels worse than standing in a corner. He should have friends his age. But none of them go out anymore. After the funeral, he declined all the dinner offers and soon they stopped inviting him. They were mostly Jennifer's friends. He has never been good at socializing.

A round of dark brown shots appears on the table. He can't remember her name but she picks one up for him and pours it into his mouth. It tastes like cough syrup. He washes it down with the rest of his beer.

"I'll go get you another beer." Her hand now moves onto his crotch as she gently pushes herself up to stand. She's sweet. His body is relaxing.

She's back with a selection of drinks for the group. How does she manage to carry all of that with her slender fingers? His hand is on her back. It spans over one entire shoulder blade. He starts rubbing and moves it down to the exposed area between her top and jeans. Her skin is soft and inviting. His large fingers worm their way down underneath her underwear. She continues to speak to her friends as though nothing is out of the ordinary. They're laughing about their school days. Cathleen was at school with all of them. He pulls his hand out and sees the yellow gold of his wedding band. How much cash could he get for it? He hates himself. She pours another shot into his mouth. This time some of it spills out. She licks around his mouth. He grabs the back of her head and shoves his tongue into her mouth. His hand wraps around her and clumsily rubs between her thighs. She grinds her pelvis against his then laughs and moves his hand away and turns back to her friends. They roll their eyes at her and she laughs some more. It feels like a cruel laugh.

The bar has emptied and the music has been turned off. Insensitive lights expose him.

Jennifer always took care of him.

The girl stands up and smiles at him. "Don't forget your card at the bar, Mr. Joseph."

He struggles onto his feet and sways toward the bar.

"Can I pay my bill?" His speech is slurred.

"Just sign here." It's over a thousand rand.

"This is wrong. I only had one more beer."

"Your daughter ordered on your tab. Here you go."

Fuck.

He signs it and turns to look for her.

They're all gone. He's alone under fluorescent lights. It smells of cigarettes and sick. His eyes are wet as he walks to his car. It's all alone at the bottom of the street.

"Your car is safe, sir." Of course the car guard would still be here. Another person who wants to take his money. He drives off without tipping.

# 15

# FLORA
## Clear fingerprints are hard to find

Zilindile has finally fallen asleep. He is on a short pile of blankets formed into a makeshift mattress in the living room. When he sleeps, she can see that he's her child. The frown that regularly glares at her from between his eyebrows has vanished. His legs are tucked in toward himself and his right arm rests over his head.

He's safe like this, her curled-up little worm. For a moment, she wants to pick him up and rock him in her arms. That was how she used to deal with his upsets when he was a little boy. Now she's lost. How could he have grown this much? She sits next to him, stroking his forehead. They hardly touch anymore but when he's like this, she can still mother him.

She's been waiting to speak to her mother alone, since they arrived. The walls are so thin, no matter where you are you can join in someone else's conversation. It might as well be sheets dividing the two rooms. She had to wait until she was certain he was asleep. A talk between mothers should never involve a child.

But here he is, her son, his body rising and falling in naturally perfect timing that she doesn't want to leave.

She can't remember the last time she asked anyone for advice. But this is too big for her. Zilindile is vanishing and the more she tries to hold onto him, the faster he fades. He is practically a grown man. She knew the time would come when she would have to let go, when he wouldn't let her hold on any longer. But she can't allow that time to be now. He needs her.

She walks into the other room to find her mother, but the old woman is already snoring like a crocodile. They'll have to talk in the morning. She turns the light out and climbs into the bed next to her mother. It's familiar. The smells of growing up surround her, camphor cream with a hint of coconut. The smell of running from her mother's ever-ready hand. She used to give her mother headaches, especially when it came to boys. She was regularly sneaking out with different troublemakers from the neighborhood.

There was a great deal of coconut-scented slapping.

She throws her arm around the bony body next to her.

Zilindile must be careful when it comes to girls. She's always been worried about the type of man he would become.

If she's honest, she thought she would be dealing with girl trouble sooner than this. If his father, Paul, was still around, maybe things would have been different. The only version of a father Zilindile has had is Frank. What kind of example is that? A man who can't cope without a woman doesn't give the right impression of manhood.

Men must be strong and dependable, ready to bounce back from anything.

Zilindile was small enough to fit into her arms when Paul left.

Her mind won't stop working. She gets out of bed and looks for her phone. One game of *Snake 2* and she's certain everything will settle, she'll be asleep in no time. Her purse is in the kitchen, more like a short passage than a real room.

There are new tiles on the kitchen wall, yellow with white flowers. She gave her mother the money to do the tiles. They're strange, too secure for this home. Rich outsiders, showing the rest of the house just how run down it really is.

Her phone is on the work surface. The counter is marked by lines and scratches deep enough for grains of rice to get stuck in them, taunted by the new tiles.

There is an envelope sign on her phone screen.

She takes three steps into the living room and sits on the plastic covered sofa next to Zilindile and opens the message.

*Hello dear Flora. I hope you are happy. You were butiful in your white dress. This is my phone. Runyararo.*

She re-reads the message again and again. Each time, her smile spreads further across her face. She doesn't know whether to sit or stand. Zilindile is sleeping right in front of her. This message is the most intimate encounter she's had in years. She turns her back to Zilindile for privacy and begins to type a response.

*Yes. I am happy.* She deletes it and starts again. *Runyararo! Nice to hear your voice.* But she hasn't. That's terrible. He can't speak but she's imagined his voice to be deep and grainy. *Hi. I miss you.* No. Too forward. She doesn't want to sound too eager. *Hello. Thanks for your message. I am happy.* Simple and to the point. It will do.

She closes her eyes and hits the send button. A red cross appears next to the SMS. There is not enough airtime to send the message.

Zilindile's phone is lying next to him. He won't notice if she sends one message. She sneaks toward him, trying to be as quiet as possible. This is a moment to behave like a woman, not a mother.

If Zilindile wakes up, mother is all she'll be. His phone is much more complicated than hers. Why must they make these things so complicated to use?

Finally, she finds the messages. *Hello Runyararo. Nice to get your message. No airtime on my phone. Flora.* It sends. Not a perfect message. A little stained with motherhood, but it will do.

Her body bends as slowly as her joints will allow as she puts the phone back where it was.

It beeps.

She stares at her son. He doesn't move. What would he do if he woke up and found her flirting on his phone? He hasn't seen her with a man before. How would he react?

Damn, why didn't she tell Runyararo to reply to her phone? One more message and then she'll be done. Her heart is beating so hard, she's scared it'll wake Zilindile. She rushes to open the message. *Hi Zee. Soz 2 send this so L8. Bt I made it home fine! Tx 4 asking! I bn meaning 2 tell u 4 a while now bt wsn't sure how. I took a test + I'm pregnant.* Flora closes the message and puts the phone down.

This is impossible. It must be that Indian girl. She is going to be a grandmother. They will have to get married. What do Indians do in their culture? Must they pay damages? Why an Indian girl? He could easily have found a good Zulu girl. Indians are such racists.

The message could be from a different girl. Maybe he has more than one girlfriend. What if there are other babies out there? He doesn't have a proper job. Who is going to put food on the table? Who is going to buy nappies? The girl didn't look like she had much sense. Flora is going to have to pay for this baby now. Zilindile is too young for this. He could do things with his life. She should have warned him about girls. There are too many out there looking for a husband. They will try anything. How can they be sure it's his baby? They must demand proof before it goes any further. Where will the mother and baby stay? Mr. Joseph will never allow them all to stay in the back room. She sits down on the floor next to her son.

Tonight he can sleep and be her baby but tomorrow everything will be different.

The smell of porridge wakes her. For a moment she forgets where she is but as she opens her eyes she sees a pile of blankets. What was Zilindile's bed is now a neat pile of brown and green. He and his grandmother are talking in the kitchen. They are laughing about Flora sleeping on the floor. It's hard for her to sit up. Her age is announcing itself. Her bones are sore from not being on a mattress. Standing up slowly, she stretches herself out and walks to the kitchen. Zilindile almost knocks her over as he speeds to leave the room when he sees her.

"And now?"

"Sorry, Ma." His voice is more shaky than his words and she can sense his readiness to fight.

Her mother hands her a bowl of porridge. It is warm and sugary.

"Why were you sleeping on the floor like a cockroach?"

Flora shakes her head and starts to eat. Her mother pours boiling water into a bucket and carries it into the room to wash.

"Your boyfriend SMS'd you." Zilindile startles her, sending porridge down the wrong pipe. She starts coughing, spluttering porridge all over. He gets her some water. A stupid smile crawls across his face.

One good klap will get rid of that. When did he get so cheeky? "He said he thinks you're very sexy."

Did Runyararo really say that? Sexy! No one has ever called her that before. Now it's coming out of her son's mouth.

"Zilindile!" She wants to see the message.

"He wants to know when he can see you again. What I want to know is what you were doing with my phone?" He puts earphones into his ears. Children of today are ungrateful. He'll know what it's like soon enough. "I'm going back home." His bag is already on his shoulder. She tries to hold onto him, but he shrugs her off with too much ease.

"Don't go. Please..." He walks out.

She runs into the bedroom and starts flinging things into her bag.

"Have you gone mad?"

"Zilindile walked out, Ma."

"Just leave him. He must be a man. You make him a baby. Too much interfering."

"Ma, you don't know what's been happening. I must go."

"Hmm. Now you are being a baby. You won't catch him and you are too dirty to be running around the streets. Wash yourself properly, get dressed and then you can go find him. Both of you must be calm. Don't forget what happened with that Paul of yours. I don't know how many times I tried to warn you." Flora's mother clicks her tongue. "Zilindile's a good boy but he's got too much of his father in him."

Flora's mother is always crawling into her business. "And what's this about you having a boyfriend? Hmm? You are too old for those things now. You want to make a fool of yourself again?"

# 16

# CATHLEEN
*Shedding the present continuously*

Her lips are cracked granadilla skins. Tough, fading purple segments. Tightness spreads across her eyes. They are hard and dry like cement contact lenses. Her eyelids inch open for flashes of time, across the scratchy edges of her eyes. They fall shut, closing out the recurring image. Cardboard boxes, on top of cardboard boxes, next to cardboard boxes. Stiffness pulls tightly through her body. She is leaden. If only she could roll over.

The room is dry and claustrophobic. Surely too small to be a warehouse. The boxes don't change.

She focuses all her energy on one side of her body, willing it to turn over.

It won't.

Darkness returns.

*Her father wants to borrow some clothes. She hands him piles of clothes that grow from her feet. The clothes turn into a long scarf. Layers of material in a variety of colors grow straight out from where her feet were. She keeps draping them around her father. Circling him with the growing wool. Her arms are getting tired but she doesn't stop. His head pokes out of a mountain. Eventually the colors blend and there is only a gray mound. She tries to climb it but stumbles and falls into the folds of cloth. Hard, bristled fabric tears at her skin. Her hands fight to move through it. She has to find him. Her bleeding hands turn the mound into a red mess. She can't break into it.*

*Where is he?*

The box in front of her has a star drawn onto it. A solitary star, separated from the solar system with a purple marker. Her skirt has risen up. The button on it presses down into her skin. Her underwear is exposed to the rest of the room. If only she could pull her skirt down. Her arms can't move. Where is her phone? Has anyone noticed that she's missing? How long has it been? Someone must have realized by now. Flora would notice.

Her legs have turned solid. Wooden planks that extend into splinters, gashing through her toes. There is a glass of water in front of her. Through the water the star is blurred.

Her head is too heavy to lift.

Who brought the water? Has someone found her?

She hears footsteps leaving the room. Who was in here? Who saw her exposed like this? Why did they leave?

Her mouth is lined with sores. If only she could get hold of the glass. She tries to swing her arm but it only moves slightly. She tries again, pleading with her shoulder to move. Her body rocks from left to right. The relief of the button on her skirt lifting off her skin is short lived, before it presses down again. She finally manages to swing at the glass. It falls and breaks into two large pieces and hundreds of tiny shards. The water runs toward her.

She licks at it, sucking up as much as she can around the broken pieces of glass.

The star is clear again. Her limbs start to tingle, as if there are ants crawling under her skin.

She closes her eyes. The water seeps under her head and makes the concrete floor colder.

A bright light shines into her face. Someone is stroking her hair. Soft warm strokes.

When she was little and Flora put her to sleep, Flora would run her hand over Cathleen's face and hair, over and over. It smelled like Sta-soft.

She is on a carpeted floor with a blanket over her body. Where is she? There's a sandwich about a meter from her face. White bread with what looks like cheese and tomato on a chipped beige plate. There are no windows in this room. A table and a single wooden chair are at the opposite end of the room. Why has she been moved?

The smell of damp in the room mixes with the urine and sweat smells coming from her body. The pungent mixture doesn't distract her from trying to get closer to the food. Why won't her limbs work?

"You ready to talk yet? I'm sure you don't want to be difficult."

A voice from behind her head shocks her.

She opens her mouth but struggles to speak. Her throat feels scratched, like what it must feel like to swallow a prickly pear whole. The food is brought closer to her but it's still out of her reach. Her mouth starts to fill with saliva. She sees pointed shoes and the edge of neatly tailored black trousers.

"Dina! Bring me some water." He crouches down. She sees Lionel's clear blue eyes. He smiles warmly at her. She looks past him at the sandwich. The door opens and someone she can't see hands him a glass of water. He puts the glass to her mouth and helps her to drink. She is gulping hard. Water rushes around her mouth and down her throat. She could choke. He steps backwards and almost stands on the sandwich. She opens her mouth to warn him. "Oh, I'm sorry. Did you want to eat this?"

She tries to nod. He lifts half of it up toward his mouth and takes a bite. "It's not bad." He holds the sandwich out toward her. "Here you want a bite?" She moves as far as she can but doesn't reach him. Finally he tosses it down at her. Her head is close to it. She can smell the bread. All she has to do is open her mouth and bite in.

"Cathleen, you are not looking too good. I mean it's not like you were ever going to be a model, but this bad ..." He shakes his head and laughs. "It's a little pathetic, really. Do you know that you shat yourself?"

Her head is down. She chews as fast as she can, taking bites before swallowing the previous one.

"A nice hot bath would do you good. Would you like that?"

She finishes the part of the sandwich that he gave her and turns to stare at the other half on the plate. "Want some more?" She looks up at him. "Well, all I need is for you to give me one small piece of information. Then we can get you a proper bed, meals, anything you want, darling. The world is yours for the taking."

His voice is earnest. "How does that sound?"

She tries to swing her arm at the sandwich. He picks up the plate, forcing her to look at him. "What I need to know is where you live."

"I?" Her voice is raspy.

"Do you want some more water?" She nods. "Where do you stay?"

"Home...my dad."

"Are you trying to fuck with me? You think that's clever?" He takes a bite of the sandwich.

"Please. No. Sorry." Why is he doing this?

"Then, where is your house?"

Why does he want to know? Her family is there. She's silent. He'll hurt them. Tie them up and kill them. Or bring them all here? What is this?

He kicks her. His foot drives into her stomach. It feels like all the oxygen in her body has strained out of her pores. This must be what happens when a window is broken inside an airplane. Blood rushes to her head. It's full. She can't take anything in.

He kneels down next to her and grabs her by the hair. He yanks her to her feet. Strands of hair are pulled from her scalp.

He releases her.

She crumples to the floor. It's worse than the kick. Shooting pains spread through her body.

His hand is in her hair again. He jerks her up.

"Please, don't."

"Then tell me. Where do you live?"

She opens her mouth and closes it again.

He drops her. It feels like her bones might split. She is crumpled like a used tissue. He reaches his hands back into her hair.

"Park...Parkview. I live in Parkview." He pulls her up.

"Where exactly?"

"Please..." He punches her in the stomach. She feels dizzy. "It's 110...Kilkenny..." She's sobbing. "Kilkenny Road in Parkview."

"Good girl. Was that really so hard? Here you go." He pours some more water into her mouth. "What's the code for the alarm?"

He pulls the glass back.

She chokes as he drops her. "The alarm isn't working."

"Are you going to lie to me? Is that smart, do you think?"

"I'm not. It's broken. I promise."

"We'll know soon enough, won't we?"

"Please, don't hurt them, please, my dad, my...James."

He leaves the room.

What do they want with her family? What has she done? She should've bought time. She could've given the wrong address. Why didn't she think about that? They probably have her house keys. James doesn't deserve this. She should have protected him. He's still just a little boy, hasn't been in a real fight or anything. She always thought that James was going to be the one to do something with his life.

Dina comes back into the room. She puts a hand under each of Cathleen's armpits and starts to drag her out. Cathleen starts crying. She sees the other half of the sandwich moving further away from her.

Where is this woman taking her? What more could they possibly want from her? She is blubbering and feels light under Dina's firm grip.

"Fucking shut up already. You're stinking like a rabid dog, in need of a good cleanup." She pulls Cathleen down the passage, past different doorways. It looks like a house but not one that anyone lives in. There is hardly any furniture and most of the light bulbs need replacing.

Dina drops Cathleen on the bathroom floor. Her head is below the toilet seat. "You need to lose some weight, little pig." Dina is breathing heavily and rests against the peeling bathroom door before placing Cathleen in the bath. The tub is more brown than white. She sprays cold water onto Cathleen's clothed body. The water pressure is hard and beats at her limbs. She lifts each of Cathleen's arms and sprays underneath them and then faces the showerhead in between Cathleen's legs.

Cathleen wants to close them but they won't move. Nothing will.

The purple star is back. It stares at her. Most of her body is dry but her clothes are slightly damp. She stretches her mouth open and the skin on her top lip tears. A fine cut appears. A trickle of blood runs into her mouth.

# 17

# FARHANA
*Swallowing into the vacuum*

The smell of frying onions, garlic and chilies fills the house. The entire family has been growing increasingly excited for tonight. They are waiting to check the moon, to find out if Eid is tomorrow or the next day. Her mother has already stockpiled food in the freezer. Plastic bags filled with different types of samoosas and pies take up all the remaining space in there. The sweetmeats—chana magaj, jalebi and burfi—are ready on platters wrapped with plastic and ribbons, waiting to be taken to the neighbors on Eid day.

Today could be the last day of fasting; soon life will return to normal. They will all fatten up and be refreshed at work. Farhana has secretly been eating the whole day. Her mother sent her to the shops earlier to buy butter and milk for tonight and she decided to buy some snacks for herself. Pregnant women aren't supposed to fast. How will she tell them that she's pregnant?

It will have to wait until after Eid. To expose such a sin during Ramsaan, when even the most immoral Muslims tend to take on religious fervor, feels worse than if it were any other time.

There is a miniature feast on her bedroom floor. She is surrounded by gums, chocolate, chips and a jam donut. Her mother would die if she walked in right now. She picks up the donut and bites into it. The sugar clings to the corners of her mouth as apricot jam erupts from the top. She places her mouth over the jam and sucks the thick syrupy goo out. The possibility of mess is avoided and she devours the rest of it in four large bites.

Her stomach turns. She's feeling ill and hides the rest of her goodies underneath the bed.

"Farhana! How many times must I ask you to set the table?" Her mother is insanely irrational when she's fasting. There are still two hours left before they can start eating. But Farhana doesn't want to argue and risk the chance of her mother coming in and finding her sugar-coated mouth. She has to be on her best behavior until she tells them about her pregnancy.

"Okay Mummy. I'm going to do it now now." She slips into the bathroom and rinses her hands and face. Laying the table is usually calming. The simplicity of it allows her time for contemplation.

Today the thoughts are stressing her out. With each plate she lays, she thinks of another relative, someone else who will be disappointed in her. She thinks of Uncle Samad. She imagines his reaction. His eyes will widen and his beard will stop its bobbing before his temper takes over. It could rise in minutes. What if he decides to throw her out of her mother's house? In this family his word is almost as sacred as the Qur'an.

She can't tell them. She's heard the gossip about families whose daughters these things happen to. Her family prides themselves on finishing university, getting married and living like good Muslims. She would be the first to bring any kind of disrepute to them.

Something has to be done.

There is only one computer in the house. It's on a small desk in the corner of the lounge. A red office chair is neatly tucked under the school desk. The computer is old and the internet is depressingly slow. Fortunately, her mother is too busy in the kitchen to check up on her. The house is small enough for Farhana to hear her mother talking to herself about which spices go into each dish.

Finally the internet connects. She looks around the room, then types "abortion" into Google and listens for her mother in the kitchen before pressing enter. The search brings up a combination of explanations, clinics and fundamentalist groups strongly against abortion. Her mother is shouting at the cumin for hiding. Farhana clicks on a link to a clinic. There is a picture of a hammock with a sunset behind it. Why have they made this clinic look like a day spa?

She checks her phone. Zee hasn't contacted her since she told him.

The site continues to describe the process of abortions with words like "mifepristone", "progesterone" and "methotrexate." It sounds like a science textbook. Where is the price?

Her mother is quiet. The hairs on the back of Farhana's neck perk up. "Mummy? You okay?" Her fingers are ready to exit the internet.

"Stupid, bloody chicken. Why did you have to go and burn? What is wrong with you!"

Farhana opens a new tab on the *Financial Mail*, just in case someone does walk in. She returns to her original search. There's plenty of information but it's not what she needs. Where is the price? Surely they should put that first. *Don't bother to read further if you don't have X amount!*

She looks at the door. Beads of sweat start to run down her forehead. She grabs a piece of paper and scribbles down the number. The computer really should be in her room. She's the only one who uses it.

"What a beautiful roti you are." Once her mother starts heating the rotis, she knows that the preparation for supper is almost done.

The next website she opens has a pop-up advert on the side with a picture of a blue-eyed baby. Who advertises baby products on the side of an abortion website?

She can't hear her mother anymore and shuts down the page.

It was stupid to Google abortions at home in the first place. At least she has one phone number. She's not even sure what she wants to do. How does anyone make this decision? If only she could speak to Zee. There is no one that she can talk to. Who would understand? If she keeps the baby, what will she do about university? It might still be possible to finish this year. Unless her mother forces her to have a rushed marriage before anyone thinks otherwise. She's not ready to get married and Zee is a drug dealer. There will be no house, no future. How is she going to explain that she had sex with a drug dealer? How is she going to explain that she had sex at all? Her mother has never spoken about sex. What kind of a father would Zee make? She wouldn't be able to depend on him to get a real job. He would probably just take the baby with him to sell drugs. He's a liar. He lied about everything. And he's black. How will her mother handle that? There's no good spin to put on it. She's pregnant with a domestic worker's son, who has matric but whose skill is drug peddling.

How did she get herself into this?

"Farhana! Open your ears. Somebody by the door."

"Salaam Uncle."

"Salaam." His beard has more fervor than usual. It points at her as though it can smell her shame. "Mummy still in the kitchen?"

"Gee, Uncle." He takes a seat in the lounge. Why doesn't he go to the kitchen and talk to her mother? Now she has to sit here and be scrutinized by him.

"So, when does university start again?"

"Next week."

"Such long holidays. At least you'll get to have a nice long relax in front of the TV after Eid. These days you children work too hard. Too much stress. It's good to have a break. You know, just the other day I was reading about these children who are killing themselves from all the stress. You must enjoy this time. Kick off your shoes and lay back. Soon you will be a chartered accountant making the big bucks and your mother and I can do the relaxing." He laughs to himself.

If she has this baby, no one will be relaxing or becoming a CA any time soon. "You know that Farouk's daughter. What was her name? Ayesha or Ani...something, I can't remember. But she just finished her studies and married a lovely boy. Pharmacist, I think. They—"

"Farhana, come help dish up."

"Excuse me, Uncle." She is out the door before he can say anything else.

More people start arriving as the food is dished into serving bowls. Uncle is busied with opening the door and sharing his readings with whichever unfortunate soul sits next to him. She is happy to be carrying food into the dining room and avoiding conversation with any of the family.

At last everyone is seated and about to tuck in, when her cellphone starts to ring. *Fuck you ooh ooh*...She must change her ringtone. *And fuck you too*, sings out from the kitchen. It might be Zee.

Uncle stares at her as though he is daring her to go and answer it in the middle of supper....*ooh ooh ohh*. The rest of the family keeps uncharacteristically silent, looking at each other as though they are asking if they heard the words correctly. She receives a variety of disapproving looks. Her uncle is probably going to come up with some story about how cellphones are destroying the youth. She keeps herself glued to her chair. Everyone knows it's her phone but getting up isn't an option. Finally, the ringing stops and they begin chatting again.

After dinner, she clears the plates and rushes into the kitchen to check her phone. It was Zee. He probably needed time to wrap his head around things. She should've remained calm.

"Farhana, stop playing with your phone. Who was phoning you at that time?"

"Some girl from university, Mummy."

"Why was she calling at Iftar time?"

Farhana shrugs.

"Go and find out if anyone needs drinks."

"Okay Mummy." Farhana escapes to the lounge and comes back with an array of orders.

Once they all have their teas and coffees, she rushes to her room to listen to Zee's message.

*Hey babe, it's me. Got back from my gran's place. Anyway, there's a massive party tonight. I can come and get you. Let me know.*

That's it. How can he expect her to go out when she's pregnant! Not a single word about the lies. Nothing about what happened with his mother at the house.

She is too angry to call him. She texts instead. Not up to it.

*What's with you Zee? You need to grow the fuck up.* She glares at the phone, challenging it to respond.

It doesn't.

"Farhana, we can't see the moon! We'll be fasting one more day."

One more day. The last day of hiding. She will tell her mother after Eid.

# 18

# RUNYARARO

*The enamel barriers*

They're on their way back to Lionel's. The houses they pass look like traps. The promising gates and entrances are bait, drawing in dreams and locking them up behind burglar bars. Earning money in this way won't provide any sense of calm. He'll be stuck, either in one of these houses or in jail.

Shuvai's silence has become more apparent. They walk fast, eyes focused and hearts beating. So far they've only had to do deliveries.

But Runyararo can't stop thinking about the possibility of being asked to do a special job. That would get them an extra thousand at the end of the week. They are already deep in over their heads but Shuvai convinced him to finish the week. At least they will have some money to survive until he can find them other work. What if a special job comes up before then?

A black rat crosses their path. It is as large as a small cat—its belly swollen. As it crosses the road Runyararo notices that it's as quick-witted as it is filthy, hustling between the cars in a back and forth sort of dance, untroubled by the danger its life is in. It is about to reach the other side. It stops. Its nose is twitching. It turns back to look for whatever its nose has picked up. A taxi swerves to a stop and traps it under its front wheel. Its belly bursts. None of the passengers getting on or off the taxi notice it at all.

What if a special job means killing someone? If they don't do it, Lionel might kill them. They know his face, his name and where he runs his business from. He won't just let them go home. Runyararo prays that today will be a normal delivery. The past few days have been any-thing but normal. His driving has improved and he has started feeling less edgy but every time they leave in that Golf, packed with whatever it is they're carrying, he knows that it could be the last time he's free.

They're at the black gate. He is tempted to place his hand on the multi-colored broken glass on the wall and press down until it can no longer be used. If your hands don't work, you can't be asked to kill someone.

Shuvai rings the bell and implores Runyararo to go inside with him. They know where to go now and head straight to the storeroom with the boxes.

"Hey! Where do you think you going?" It's Dina, standing outside Lionel's office. "You're not delivering today. Boss has got another job for you two." Runyararo doesn't want to hear about any other job. If he runs now, what will they do? He could disappear by tomorrow.

"Come in here. Now! Stop behaving like fucking retards."

Lionel is sitting in his chair. Runyararo's heart jumps into his throat. They haven't seen him since the day they started working. He is wearing a gray suit with a plain white shirt and a yellow tie. The yellow makes his pale blue eyes look ghostly.

"Come in, gentlemen. Tell me, how have things been going?"

"Uh, fine Mr....fine."

Shuvai should tell him now. This is the perfect time. They don't know enough to be killed yet. They haven't ever looked inside the boxes.

Runyararo shakes his head.

"Well...Mr. Silent? Why are you shaking your head?"

Runyararo blinks at Lionel.

"What's the problem with him?"

Shuvai looks at Runyararo, pleading.

"No. Nothing. He's just...uh...grateful for the job, sir."

Shuvai's legs are shaking.

"Okay. This is an important job now, not just lifting and carrying."

They're too late to pull out now. They're going to become murderers.

"This is the address. Here are the house keys."

Shuvai is going to have to do the killing.

"I've been assured there is no alarm. You shouldn't have any problems. Wait until the man leaves the house before you go in. There are two floors. You go upstairs," he points at Shuvai. "Check for jewelry, watches, electronics—anything worth selling. There might be a safe, so keep an eye out.

"Mr. Silent, you do downstairs. I want computers, the TV, printers, iPods, iPads and any cash you can find. These people are stinking rich. There should be plenty. This is a special job, gentlemen. You know what that means for you.

"Be quick and quiet. And remember I know what's in the house, so don't try to be clever and pocket any of the stuff.

"Bring it here when you're done."

"Thank you, sir."

Is Shuvai out of his mind? They could have explained to the police before that they were ignorant delivery men, but there's no way to explain stealing. It's not murder but it still means jail time.

A man comes into the room. It's the man they delivered to in Hyde Park.

"We done with this one yet? I think I found another last night." He addresses Lionel.

"Almost." Lionel looks irritated with the long-face man. "Thanks gentlemen. You can go." They head out. Lionel's voice booms through the thin door. "How many times must I tell you? Watch what you say!"

Runyararo is happy not to be in the room. "Turn right here. Look, man, I know you're upset but we'll get paid tomorrow and then we'll be done with this. I promise. Take another right at the stop street. Think about it, R2200 each!"

Runyararo glowers at him. This is the problem with hanging around younger people, they don't think!

"I should have said something about quitting earlier. I know. Left at the second traffic lights. I was scared, man. What did you want me to do?"

Runyararo keeps his eyes focused on the road.

"You should have said something, then. Fuck you, old man! You owe me. You know that? I got you all your jobs, since you got here. You think I want to babysit some old retard every day?"

Runyararo stops the car. He opens the door and steps outside.

"What are you doing, man?"

Runyararo struggles to take in the icy air. His chest is constricted. He lifts his arms up to the sky and leans back against the car.

"Please, get back in." Shuvai's voice drowns in the buzzing stream of passing cars. Runyararo has stopped in an inconvenient place. People curse and hoot at them as they drive by. Runyararo takes it all in. He deserves it. He wants to get the guilt beaten out of him. A few smacks from his mother used to do the trick when he was young.

His phone beeps.

He gets back into the car and reads the message. *I am taking my son to church today. When can I see you? Flora.*

*Soon. After tomorrow. I'm missing you.* He could use the money to get Flora something really fancy. Spend it all at once and then he can be done with this business.

He starts the car again.

"That's it, man! I've had it. You're crazy. After this…You and me, we done man. See how easy it is to look after yourself."

Runyararo gives him a silencing look and snatches the address from Shuvai's hand: 110 Kilkenny Road, Parkview. It can't be.

"Look, I'm sorry, man. I knew you wouldn't want to do this. And especially not here at Flora's place. But it won't take long. Let's just get through it."

They stop a few houses up the road, where they can just see number 110. Runyararo types a message for Shuvai to read. *Tomorrow you tell Lionel we going back to Zim for a funeral and we can't work. Then we disappear.*

"That's a great idea, man. Wait here. I'm going to check if the man's car is there." Shuvai attempts to walk as calmly as possible but Runyararo can see that his hands are tapping against his thighs. He is moving like a crab, small shifts to the right and then back to the left.

*Flora, how long are you going to be at church? When will you be back at home?* Please let her reply soon. Shuvai is walking back to the car.

"His car is still there, we have to wait."

The neighborhood is quiet. The purple trees branch out and over the street in a protective way, as though they are keeping the noise out, watching over people's homes. Their roots hold firmly onto the earth below.

Runyararo sees Mr. Joseph come outside and open the garage. The big man hunches his shoulders so much it looks like he is trying to hide from the world. Runyararo checks his phone. Flora still hasn't responded.

"You ready? Sorry. Stupid question. We better park inside so no one sees the car." Shuvai jumps out and runs over to the gate and tries the keys. He strikes it lucky on the second attempt.

Runyararo stares at him from the car. Shuvai is waving him in but he can't start it. His body mimics his voice. Everything is in working order but refuses to do the job. He should drive away. The car must be stolen and Lionel wouldn't risk calling the police. He could drive to Durban or Cape Town, anywhere but here.

What about Flora? He could take her with him but then he needs to get paid first. He starts the car and speeds into hiding. Shuvai shuts the gate behind him. Runyararo doesn't want to get out of the car but he knows that he has to rush, in case Flora comes home. She can't find him there. If she finds out how he got the money she will never look at him in the same way again.

Shuvai heads upstairs, leaving him at the bottom of the staircase. He never ventured this far into the house when he worked here. They didn't check if either of the children is at home. What if the girl sees him? Her words are coming true.

He stands in the lounge, surveying what needs to be taken. The vase that Mr. Joseph kept checking for the money is right in front of him. This is his chance to get retribution. If he hadn't been falsely accused, none of this would be happening. It's their fault. He picks up the vase, lifts it above his head and then puts it down again. There's no time for nonsense. And besides, it wasn't the vase's fault and Flora would be the one forced to clean it up.

"Come on, man." Shuvai gives him such a fright he swings around and his elbow knocks the vase to the floor.

It shatters. What was once whole is now nothing but fragments.

They get everything that they can fit into the Golf and are out and on the road in minutes.

Blood races through Runyararo's body. He drives as fast as he can.

"South Africans think they have wealth, man. This is nothing. You remember the white people's houses in Mutare. A village of servants was needed for each home." Shuvai is shaking but his eyes are fiercely alive.

It was strangely liberating to retaliate against the Joseph family. The day they called him a thief they didn't realize they were calling it into being. He doesn't know whether he's excited or horrified.

There are cars all around them, hooters going and music blaring. He wants to speed but they don't need to attract any attention to themselves. The last thing they need right now is to be pulled over by a traffic cop. He stops at red lights and only accelerates in quiet residential areas.

Dina lets them in and shows them where to put the stuff. How many empty rooms do they have in this place?

"Okay. So? Any problems?" Her grubby fingers pick through the objects.

"No. It was fine."

"Come by tomorrow for your pay and I think there's a delivery for five o'clock, so you must be here by four at the latest."

"We will. Is uh...Mr. Lionel going to be here?"

"How the hell do I know?"

# 19

# FRANK
## When the ball slips the floor is near

The gate is open. Did he forget to close it? Trying to jog his memory is becoming more and more impossible. It was probably Cathleen. She can be so irresponsible. She's always incapacitated when she gets home and forgets to do the simplest things.

There are many things they need to talk about. They should've gone to therapy after Jennifer's death but he was in no state to think rationally. Cathleen is slipping through his fingers. He has let go for too long. He can't remember the last time they were in the same room. Probably that time they fired the painter, over a week ago.

The gate looks like an open mouth welcoming the outside world. Hopefully she's at home. He needs to talk to her. He has wanted to tell her about the plan to move, but they've been coming and going around each other. There's no point in waiting until three in the morning for her to come home—then she'd be too drunk to talk.

He pulls his car into the garage, gets out and closes the gate.

Walking back along the side of the car, he steps on something. It's a cellphone. A cheap one. Probably belongs to one of the kids' friends. These children don't know how to look after anything. He picks it up and walks inside.

The house looks different but he can't quite put his finger on it. Flora sometimes rearranges the furniture. Maybe it's that. He goes over to the fridge and grabs a cold beer before heading to the TV room. The house has a strange smell, like it is someone else's home. He can't usually smell his own house. He can't pinpoint exactly what the difference is but it's odd. He sits down and stares at the empty space on the wall where the TV used to be. Wait.

It takes a few seconds before he understands what has happened. Fuck.

How did they get in? Are they still inside?

"Cathleen, are you home?" He is on his feet, bounding up the stairs to the bedrooms. Her bed is made. In fact everything is neatly packed away. This is abnormal. At least she wasn't here. Her desk is empty.

That's one laptop gone.

He rushes into James's room. James is away until tomorrow. Thank heavens no one was home. He stalks around the house, bending his head around corners, peeping into each room. The robbers must be gone.

He walks into his bedroom, which is a complete mess. The cupboard doors are open and the paintings have been taken off the wall and placed on the floor amongst other random clutter. The dresser is open. An emerald earring is lying on the floor, a single fallen piece of Jennifer. The rest of her jewelry is gone. The dresser is now as empty as her side of the bed.

He had wanted to give Cathleen and James special pieces from her collection so that they would always have something of their mother's. Something for them to hand down to their own children one day. Cath was supposed to get the pair of earrings. He had given them to Jennifer on the day she was born and for James there was a ring. He should have done it sooner but he hadn't wanted to upset the dresser while it was still filled with Jennifer's scent. It's all gone now.

He sits on the bed and leans over and picks up the earring.

The design is simple. Three silver strands plaited into each other until they form a solid nest to house a green gem at the bottom of the earring. There's something protective about the way the silver holds the emerald.

What if the thieves come back?

He heads back downstairs to call the police. There's a station a few streets away. It shouldn't take them long to get here. He walks around the property and tries to work out how the robbers got inside. It's unsettling. There are no broken windows. The doors appear to be untouched. Besides his bedroom, not a whole lot of mess has been made. It's almost as though the thieves knew where to look. He moves around the house, not knowing where to sit or what to do. Other people were in his home. What if they had found him here? He never felt vulnerable when he was younger. His size made up for his lack of fighting skills. Now his body is hunched and old. He's turned into an easy target. The space is teeming with memories of Jennifer. It hasn't been easy to live here since she died. No one sits on her chair at the dinner table. No one sits at the dinner table at all. The space next to his on the couch became cold. It's the most well preserved part of the old couch. After the funeral, the house became a safe space, somewhere to get away from pitying eyes and the hugs of strangers. His home, filled with all his recollections, has been violated. It's a crime scene. Nothing feels like his anymore. It's been altered. Privacy has been replaced by gaping holes. He paces up and down the passage between the lounge and the kitchen.

This is the last straw. They have to move.

The police should have been here by now.

He decides to start making a list of all the things that are missing from his home. When they arrive, he'll have something under control. The TV, decoder and the DVD machine are gone....He hopes that none of his insurance payments lapsed. There's a good chance that the debit order didn't come off this month.

He sits down on the floor. A thin film of dust marks the areas around where the missing items used to be.

He sees Flora through the window. She is walking to her room with her son Zilindile in tow. Frank is jealous of the discipline she seems to have instilled in the boy, all on her own. He stares at the young man carrying his mother's things, a slight step behind her.

What if the thieves got into her room and are hiding there?

"Flora." He runs out toward them. She has placed her key in her door but stops to look at him.

"Yes, sir?"

"We've...We were robbed. Be careful, they might be in your room."

She is careful when opening the door. Frank realizes that he has not seen the inside of this room since she moved in about twenty years ago. It is filled with his family's castoffs. The green chair that he bought for Jennifer with the butterflies is the first thing he sees. Jennifer was polite enough to pretend to like it for a short while but he knew the meanings of her different ways of saying thank you. When he brought home that chair, she gave him a thank you that made him want to take it straight back to the shop, but she insisted that it was fine. It could stay, at least for a while. He had wondered where it had gotten to.

Flora's bed has Cathleen's old duvet cover on it and there is a mattress on the floor next to the bed. That must be where her son sleeps. They sleep in the same room, not even a meter apart. How do they manage it? Cathleen constantly complains about not having enough privacy. It's not natural for a parent and her grown child to share such a small space. Why had he not thought of this before?

He stands in the doorway, staring at fragments of his past life.

Flora lives with all of his memories.

"Is...Flora, is anything missing?"

"No. It looks the same, sir. I'll come and help you now now."

She stands inside the doorway and seems to be refusing him entry into her room. She is in his home every day but now she doesn't want him to step inside. It's still his property, after all. He tries to step toward her but sees her son unpacking grocery bags.

He doesn't want to make things any more uncomfortable. She turns her back to him and goes to switch her kettle on. She takes out two mugs. They are Frank's old mugs. It looks very domestic and intimate. For one brief moment he imagines foolishly that one might be for him but of course it is for the boy.

"I just need my cup of tea, sir. Then I will change and come and clean, sir." He takes a step back. Here is a family, living in his backyard, doing their daily rituals and getting on with their lives. There was a time when Cathleen and Zilindile would play together in the yard. She struggled to pronounce his name and eventually called him Zee. The two of them were inseparable but he doesn't know if they even talk to each other anymore.

He realizes that he has been staring and makes to leave.

"It's okay, Flora. There's no real mess that can't wait till tomorrow. I just wanted to make sure that you were okay."

"I will come inside anyway, sir. It will be better."

What will be better? She is so bizarrely calm. Surely she can under-stand the gravity of the situation. Someone was here, in the yard, in the house. She could have been at home and caught in the middle of it. She seems more concerned with her tea than anything else.

The doorbell rings.

It's the police. They walk in with a sense of authority. There are two of them, both slightly shorter than Frank but still big men. The chubbier of the two takes out a notepad and rests it on his belly. He is so out of shape that there's no way he'd be able to chase down a criminal.

"So...What happened here?"

Frank feels scrutinized.

"Can't you see? We've been robbed."

"Alright. When exactly did this happen?" The policeman slouches forward, like he's too tired to be there.

"I don't know. I wasn't home. I called as soon as I got home. Maybe an hour ago?"

"That was today, sir?" The "sir" that comes out of his mouth sounds like an insult.

"Yes. I left home at about two."

"So between two and...what time did you come back?"

"Well, it's six now. Like I said, I called about an hour ago, so be-tween two and five." The policeman writes for a long time. Occasionally stretching out his arms and then continuing to write.

"Do you want us to look around?"

What would be the point? The thieves are long gone by now.

"No. It's fine. I...just need a case number for insurance purposes."

"Have you got a table for us to use to write your statement?"

What has he been writing all this time? Frank leads him to the dining room table.

The thinner policeman walks around the house, looking at it like he's casing it for another robbery. The other one continues to write, noting down all the missing items. He is writing infuriatingly slowly. Frank wants to grab the page from him and write it himself.

"Ja. Okay, so how did they get into the house?"

"I don't know."

"Was there anybody at the house?"

"No, no one."

"And alarm? Was it on?"

"It's not working."

"Hmmm. Any broken windows?"

"If there were, I would know how they got in, wouldn't I?"

"Calm down, sir. I did not steal your things."

"No broken windows, but the gate was open when I got home."

"Ah. So you do know how they got in. You see why I must ask these questions, sir? Did you leave the gate open when you left your house?"

"No. No I definitely closed it. I'm sure I did."

The policeman finishes writing out the statement and hands it over for Frank to read and sign. He skims through it. He's tired of having these guys in his house.

"Would you like us to take fingerprints?"

"Is that going to help?"

The policeman stares at him blankly.

"No. Don't worry. Thank you. I just wanted the case number."

He walks them out. He makes sure the gate is locked behind. He tries to phone Cathleen but gets her voicemail. There's no point in worrying James while he's at a friend's place. He'll tell him when he gets back. This is another good reason to move. He starts locking up and sees the phone he found outside lying on the kitchen counter. He tries to turn it on but the battery is dead. His charger won't fit. Maybe Flora has one that will. He starts walking to the back door but stops short. He'll ask her tomorrow.

Someone is in the room. The boxes are moving. She can hear them scraping toward the door but she can't see the person. Footsteps leave the room and the door closes.

# CATHLEEN
*Single strands struggle to hold on*

Her hair has started to mat into a single clump. The thin strands have attached themselves to each other, fusing together into one knotted wad.

The door opens again. Now there are two sets of footsteps.

"Do a last quick check, man." She doesn't recognize the voice.

The door closes again, leaving a single set of footsteps. She listens to the slow steady feet making their way around the room.

"Hello?" Her voice scrapes out. The steps have stopped next to her. What is he doing here? His eyes are wide. "Please...some water." Did he bring her here?

He leaves.

The garden looks different. It has taken on a new face. She no longer sees bushes but rather the perfect hiding places for tsotsis.

Why didn't Mr. Joseph get the police to do a proper check?

## 21

# FLORA
*Hers are certain, a clearly marked map*

Zilindile has been in the bathroom for too long now. And where is Cathleen? She hasn't been home for days but Mr. Joseph doesn't look worried. Maybe Cathleen went somewhere with friends. Has she even got friends? This shouldn't be Flora's problem. She has enough on her plate with Zilindile.

The wind picks up, rattling the branches of the trees. She looks outside to see if anyone is hiding out there. Zilindile must come now. If she can sort him out, then maybe she can speak to Mr. Joseph about Cathleen.

Maybe there's nothing to worry about and he knows exactly where Cathleen is.

She stares at the woven mat at the door. Coarse fibers cross over each other with perfect symmetry, waiting to be scuffed by dirty shoes. Mud particles have fallen in between the cracks, nesting there until the one day a week when she shakes it out, ridding the welcome mat of debris. The letters spelling out the greeting, to guests who never visit, have almost completely faded. It is yet another one of the many items passed on to her from the Joseph family. It does its job just fine. But the Josephs got bored with it when they found a better one with clear hospitable letters.

She hasn't found the time to talk to Zilindile about the girl and the baby. Whenever there was a break in conversation she would chicken out and busy herself with *Snake 2*. He hasn't brought it up either. She's been hoping that he would say something first so she doesn't have to admit to reading his message.

He walks up to the door. Sunlight falls across his face, creating enough shadow for her to see the features of his father. She can't let him turn into Paul. Zilindile must take care of his child. Could he really have made a baby?

She is too old for this. Or maybe she's not old enough.

"Ma, are you okay?"

"Yes. No. I have a headache. Please bring me some water."

How can she start the conversation? What is the first thing to say? The right way to put it? Her words are cowards. She wants to look serious, the way the priest looks in church. But she still doesn't know what to say.

"Here, Ma."

She takes a large gulp. "Zilindile."

"Yebo, Mama." He looks at her expectantly. She finishes the water in two more large gulps and hands him the glass.

"Do you want more? You're thirsty today." She nods.

It might be easier if she sat on a more commanding seat. She moves to the chair with the butterflies on it. The chair doesn't help. It doesn't give her the wisdom she's looking for but Zilindile is back with the water so she stays put. The glass shakes in her hand.

"Zilindile." Her voice comes out in a higher pitch than usual.

It feels like something is strangling her throat.

"Ma?" He is starting to look worried.

"You know there are things that...well...we need to....Zilindile, I suppose I haven't..." No, she mustn't accept the blame for this. "We must be free with ourselves. Talk about things that...well, we haven't spoken about." She crosses her legs.

"What's wrong, Ma?" He twirls his dreadlocks.

She braces herself. "There are things, Zilindile. Things that are special to people." She recalls the rhythm of the priest's sermons. "We must take care of these things, protect them from evil. They are not for ...not to be abused. Gifts come our way from time to time. Sometimes they are not gifts, sometimes they are the Devil's work in disguise. So you can't just jump, because it is not yours to have."

"What are you saying, Mama? You are not making any sense. Did I break something?"

"You tell me, Zilindile? Did you break something or did you take it?" She knows she is not being clear. She needs to spit it out.

"You think I stole? Are you blaming me for what happened in the big house?"

She shakes her head.

"I was with you when it happened. But now, you've been watching me. I know. Checking the times I leave and when I come home. I see the way you are staring at me, Ma, like I'm a common thug."

"I never said you are a thief. I'm talking about that...Zilindile, certain moments in life cannot be reversed. Everything is not as simple as we would like. God challenges us. These challenges are there for us to prove our strength and our worth. When the final day comes...we can say we belong in the Kingdom of Heaven. God does forgive with an open heart and he wants us to live in his image. I am not God but I forgive you. But now...Now, you have the opportunity to do the right thing. You must be a man and take responsibility."

"If you tell me what you think I did, then maybe I can, Ma!"

He is getting impatient. His hands are tucked into his pockets but she can see them tensing into fists through his denims. Paul did the same thing. Every time he was getting ready to leave her, his fists would go straight into his pockets.

"It's my fault, isn't it? I should have been tougher. At least talked to you firmly, you never had a father to do those things and...Girls are...well...they are different. They cannot run from things. Girls are always stuck with the problems. You can't understand this. You and your father with your long fast legs, you want to leave everything. Out the door and gone. Please, Zilindile, stay put. Don't be like that good-for-nothing father of yours. That poor girl..."

"Is this about the other day in the big house, Ma? It's okay. She said it's over. She doesn't want to see me. So don't worry, it won't happen again. It's done."

"Done? Zilindile, what have we been talking about? What about the baby?"

"Baby? What are you talking about?"

"Don't lie to me. I saw your message the other night. I was waiting for you to tell me but I couldn't be patient anymore."

"Baby? Ma, I have to go!" He rushes out the door.

That's the problem with boys. They hear that word and they're gone speedier than a plane. She should have said something earlier.

Her phone is within arm's reach. *Snake 2* starts up. She's starting a new game and the snake is still a small worm. Perhaps Paul's mother went through the same thing with him. She was an awful woman. Her snake eats the food and starts growing. Down, right, down, left, more bonus bugs. Her thumb starts to feel stiff.

She must make an effort with this girl. She must go and meet her whole family. The snake keeps growing, the score is rising. What will the girl's family think of Flora? She stops the game.

# FARHANA
*The holes are filled*

Her Eid outfit is lying on the bed when she comes back from the shower. This year she decided to buy a Punjabi. It is maroon and yellow, with delicate mirrors along the neckline. Farhana and her mother went to buy it long before she knew that she was pregnant. It is still the right choice and perfect for hiding her belly. The soft cotton pants have a drawstring to adjust around her growing midsection. She ties the string into a bow over her navel.

Her stomach is like a present, wrapped in the colors of the sun.

The top is loose and flows down to her knees. The foreign smell of the new clothes drapes her in a spicy sweet mixture, as if they were dipped in incense.

She puts on some eyeliner and mascara and looks at her almond eyes. As she sees herself in the mirror, she starts to believe that she could be a mother.

Last night when she saw the new moon she held on to her mother's hand. The sky was a dark heavy blanket with the tiniest slit cut out of it. Over the course of the month the slit would grow into a full circle before being covered once again. She remembered the many times that she had seen the first peep of the moon.

When she was little, she would have her parents on either side of her, each holding one of her hands. Last night she had felt the lack of balance. She tried to remain calm but tears raced down her cheeks. Her mother remained focused on the moon; only her hardened fingers adjusted themselves between Farhana's.

Telling her about the baby might not be as bad as she imagined.

She starts to plait her hair, dividing the thick soft tresses into three equal parts. Then she lays one section over another, until they combine into one single braid down her back. She smoothes the stubborn stray hairs into place with some hair oil.

She goes into the lounge to see if there is anything left to prepare but it has all been done. The table is set and weighed down by all the steaming dishes calling out to be eaten. Her mother has outdone herself this year.

Farhana sits next to her mother on one of the couches facing the door. Her mother is luminous in a bright pink skirt and a matching blouse and stares at the door, anticipating the arrivals.

She could tell her now, while they are still waiting for the men to finish at the mosque. Soon the house will be filled with kisses, Eid Mubaraks and too many smiles to have a real conversation.

Farhana stands up and moves to the window. The street is full of children showing off their new clothes and happy to miss a day of school. Her mother closes her eyes. It was a tough Ramsaan for her this year. Age is creeping up on her. Her mother's tightly wrapped bun is thinning and her wrinkles have set deeper, like they're finally here to stay. Farhana should wait until her mother has rested properly after the stress of Ramsaan and Eid before speaking to her. It's not fair to do it now. This is supposed to be a time to rejoice. They should enjoy the feast she has spent so many hours preparing.

She decides to wait.

Two sharp knocks belt out from the door. It has begun.

The house fills quickly as people arrive in rapid succession. She moves from one embrace into another, compressed in the folds of her many overweight aunties. She is accosted by different smells and moisture levels.

"You getting nice and fat, I see." Her mother's eldest sister is pinching Farhana's side and examining her.

Farhana smiles a tight-lipped smile. Why do old people feel like they can comment freely on other people's weight? Her aunt looks like she has four stomachs in her dress, one on each side, one below her panty elastic and the biggest of all forced above her panties and flopping over.

Farhana wishes she could tell her that she's gaining weight because she wants to grow up to look just like her aunty, who doesn't know when to stop eating rotis.

The thought makes Farhana's smile more genuine.

"Come everybody, food is on the table."

The house is teeming with people today. Friends as well as family have been invited and there are children everywhere. Farhana ends up sitting with the children at the small table. She feels like a giant peering down from her stool.

If she has this baby, she will be placed at the main table. Nothing will be the same.

"Farhana." Her bearded uncle is standing in the doorway.

"Gee, Uncle?"

Then she sees him. A thin delicate face suddenly becomes visible. Zee steps out from behind her uncle. He looks young and more uncertain of himself than she's ever seen him.

What is he doing here? Has he said anything to her uncle?

She looks at Uncle Samad's face but can't read his expression. She stands up to move toward them but there are too many bodies blocking the way.

This can't be happening. She can feel her family's eyes dart between her and Zee. His skinny jeans and threadbare vest are peculiar in this setting. He is the only man without a topi.

"Hello." Her mother is talking to Zee.

"Uh, hi...mam." He is pushing his hands into his pockets.

"Mummy, this is my friend Zee...from university. I just have to give him some papers for a project we are doing together."

"Okay. Zee, is it? Why don't you sit down and have lunch first?" Zee stares at Farhana but she is also lost for words. Her uncle brings out an extra chair and seats Zee next to him at the head of the table. The food circulates and people are chatting. Luckily the children's table is close enough for her to see and hear him.

He starts dishing up but looks uncertain about how much food he should take. His plate is barely dirtied by the grains of rice he's taken.

"Don't be shy, boy." Her uncle adds more to Zee's plate.

Why must he call him boy? It's so patronizing.

"Thank you, sir."

"You also going to be an accountant, then?"

Zee looks at her.

"Uh, well..."

"Yes, Uncle. He's in my class."

"Oh, very good. Very good. Your family must be proud." Her uncle looks like he's trying to be friendly but everything he says sounds racist to her. Why should Zee's parents be proud? Would he have said that to a white boy?

"Uh, yes...I suppose so." There aren't any utensils on the table and Zee struggles to eat the rice with his fingers.

Her uncle frowns. "Farhana, go fetch a fork and knife."

"I can get it." Zee starts to stand but is stopped by her uncle's hand on his shoulder.

"No. Sit and enjoy. You're our guest today."

She sprints to the kitchen, not wanting to miss out on any of this awful conversation.

"You live close by?"

She places the cutlery next to Zee's plate. He smells clean. She loves it when he doesn't use too much deodorant. She can smell more of him. It feels like they can be closer.

"Yes. Well, no. Not too far. I live in Parkview." She hovers behind him.

"Parkview! There by Westcliff? That's a very nice area. So you drove all the way here to get some papers?" Her uncle looks back at her and raises his eyebrows to emphasize the length of the distance travelled. She scuttles back to her seat.

"Uh, ja...I mean...Yes, sir. It's quite an important project. Farhana always has the best...notes."

"I thought it was university holidays now?"

Zee looks stumped. He puts a large forkful of breyani into his mouth to give him time to think.

"It's a holiday assignment, Uncle. We have to hand it in on the first day back."

He's not her father. Why is he interrogating Zee? It's like he knows that something is not quite right.

"Zee is an interesting name. Is it short for something?"

Zee swallows hard. "Yes, uh...Zilindile."

"Zee-lin-deee-li. And what do your parents do, Zee-lin-deee-li?"

"Well my...I don't really know my dad and my mum...she works for... She's a domestic worker." He looks at Farhana.

He decides to be honest now? She stares down at her untouched plate of food.

Uncle nods.

Other topics of conversation travel across the table. She doesn't hear any of it. She tries to eat and keeps her head down. She can feel Zee staring at her.

Why did he choose to come here today of all days? The one day when everyone she knows is packed into this room. Does he think that she's already told her family? Is he here to claim the baby as his? To propose?

He has never been here in the daylight. He has never been inside her house at all. Eid is about forgiveness and moving forward but how would he even know that it's Eid? Why couldn't he have phoned first or waited in the car like he usually does?

"Your mother must be very proud of herself, getting you all the way to university and studying to be an accountant. It's very impressive, no small achievement. You know, I read something about the children of maids..." Zee looks as though he is about to correct her uncle. His bony fingers tap on the table, rattling away and attracting too much attention. "Usually, they are all mixed up. Living in someone else's big house, it confuses them and they tend to be quite lazy."

"Zee is one of the top in the class, Uncle." She regrets the lie as soon as she says it. Her family is going to find out sooner or later.

It's going to be hard to correct all of this.

"Is that so?" Zee's head moves as though it wants to nod but does an uncertain roll instead.

People start to leave the table and head into the lounge. Farhana helps to clear away the plates, stopping at her uncle and Zee. They thank her and follow the rest into the lounge. Zee looks terrified. She drops the plates in the sink, rinses her hands and rushes back to them.

Her uncle and Zee are sitting on the couch. Zee is holding onto the armrest and has swung his legs away from her uncle who has comfortably adjusted himself across the remaining space, continuing with his incessant questioning. Zee starts to pick at the threads on the couch.

"Zee, I've got those papers. Let me walk you out." She hands him a stack of her old assignments. He looks around the room and raises his hand in a half wave.

"I'll come with you." Uncle escorts them to the car. There are a few neighbors hanging around outside. Some boys hide their cigarettes behind their backs when they see Uncle. Farhana can see the smoke rising up behind them. There are people all along the street. Didn't Zee notice all this when he arrived?

Two small boys are crouched next to his car. A street-wide game of hide-and-go-seek is taking place. They run across the road and tag the safe spot on the other side.

"You know these Golfs aren't safe. Everybody wants them for the parts. I read that they are the very worst for that sort of thing. You must be careful they don't hijack you." Zee is in the car, trying to smile at Uncle.

"Okay. Thank you for lunch...and the papers."

"Drive safe now, Zee-lin-deeee-li."

# 23

# CATHLEEN
## When the pores don't allow growth

It was the painter. She's sure of it. He looked at her and left. She shouldn't have blamed him for stealing the money. This is more than she bargained for. She had just been looking for the next high. When she saw him through the window, it was like fate offering up a flashing red exit sign. She had to follow it. Nothing mattered.

She had become invisible. Her dad hadn't spoken directly to her in ages. She couldn't tell him that she took the money. He wouldn't have coped. It was the right thing to do for the family.

Her first day of school was an extraordinary day. Her dad was as excited and more nervous than she was. He told Flora to make three different types of sandwiches and added a crazy assortment of snacks. She had enough lunch to fill a small cooler box.

He took her to school. When it finished, he was there, waiting exactly where he had left her that morning. He kept his promise. It was like he had been waiting there for her all morning. She told him about everything, her teachers, her new friends and all the activities they got to do. He seemed to love it.

Now they only speak when she needs money.

The day she accused the painter, her father believed her. They were allies again, standing together against the world.

Her mother always knew the truth. She would have spotted the lie from a mile away. But she wasn't there. Her mother left them with nothing. James sometimes recounts memories that Cathleen can't remember. It's like he makes them up. Her dad allows it. He allows both of them to lie. He's too busy in his own mind to even hear them talking.

It's his fault that she's in this mess. How could he not realize what's been happening to her? He should have been a parent and grounded her. Flora would have if she could. Flora is the only one who tells James the real stories about their mother. Cathleen overheard Flora and James chatting one afternoon, the two of them were giggling in the kitchen. Cathleen had desperately wanted to be included but they just stopped talking when she walked into the room.

## 24

# FRANK
## *Hovering, a beat before kissing the floor*

"You hungry, my boy?" James is lazing on the couch, his shoes dirtying the armrest. He barely lifts his head when Frank speaks.

"Ja. Is Flora here?"

"She's in her room, I think."

"Oh. Then did you get takeaways?"

"No. I thought I'd make us something."

"Ja, right, Dad. Why don't we call Mr. Delivery rather?" These kids only know how to spend money.

"What do you feel like eating? I can make us some burgers."

James swings around to face Frank and seems to be trying to raise one eyebrow.

"Are you alright, Dad?"

"I'm fine! Now, do you want a burger or not?" James sighs and tosses himself back down on the couch. Frank starts to wish he had never made the offer.

"Ja, okay...but you never cook."

"What are you talking about? Of course I do. Remember when we were in Knysna, I cooked the whole time. Drove your mom crazy."

"But since Mom, you know...you haven't."

"Don't be silly. I have. Surely, I..." He can't think of the last time he cooked for James. It couldn't have been so long.

"I'm going to my room, call me when it's ready, Dad."

He hasn't been feeding his children. If he didn't want to tell James about moving, he wouldn't be doing it today either. He takes two beef patties out of the freezer. This isn't even real cooking. He defrosts the patties in the microwave. The bread rolls are finished so he pops some white bread into the toaster. Flora walks in as he generously butters the bread.

"Sir?"

"Flora, I thought you weren't working today?"

"I'm not, sir. I came to ask..." She stares at his hands, messily tossing the patties in the pan. The oil is too hot. They are starting to burn on the outside. A crisp dark shell, charred by the heat, keeps the meat inside from cooking through. Without any force she slips her hand around the handle of the pan and tries to move her body into his position. He allows her to take the pan but doesn't give her space. She turns the heat down a little. He looks down at her. He can see the top of her head. It's just below his armpit. His feet hold his position firmly, making it uncomfortable for her to finish the cooking. This was his meal. It was his chance to do something for his son. Why must she always be in his space? The patties are finally cooked and she turns off the stove. He takes the pan back from her and dishes up.

"What is it you wanted?" He's irritated with her.

"Sir, I want to ask...could I take leave time? Only one week. My son is having a problem. I need to fix things."

He sighs heavily. "Sorry, but it's not a good time."

"Even if I could just have the days, sir. I will come and look after James in the night time and do the dishes." He never realized how many hours she's working.

"No. There will be people coming to the house regularly. I need you to make sure it's clean. There's too much dust in this house. Look, you can take Friday off but then you need to come in early on Saturday morning. I'm having a lot of people coming on Sunday. I'm trying to sell the house."

"Sir?" She looks alarmed. He had wanted to have a proper conversation with her and discuss the situation.

"The truth is, Flora, we just don't need this much space anymore. The children are hardly at home. And it'll be better for them to be away from all of their mother's stuff. I suppose you can start looking for jobs immediately, really."

She can make a new start as well. He tries to smile at her but it's awkward. She starts to leave the kitchen. He notices the cellphone that he found is still on the table. "Flora?" She turns back toward him. How is he going to cope without her? "Do you know whose phone this is?" Shaking her head, she turns to leave. "Well, do you have a charger for it? Perhaps we can work out who it belongs to."

"I will check if mine fits. Sir...is Cathleen on holiday with friends?"

"What? No. Why?"

Flora fiddles with the phone in her hand. "Sir, she hasn't been home for long. It is many days now. Her room hasn't changed, no mess for I don't know how long, sir."

"What are you saying? Why are you only telling me this now? James! Come down here at once."

# CATHLEEN
*There is always less than before*

The door opens. He hastens toward her. There is nothing to hold onto. He crouches down. His eyes are wild as he maneuvers his hands underneath her. She tries to scratch at him. Her nails are weak and one breaks as it pierces into his skin. He folds her arms around her body like a straightjacket so that her nails can't reach him. She tries wriggling her body as much as she can but he's too strong. He grabs onto her tightly, making it impossible for her to get away. If he held on any tighter, her bones would snap.

She has never seen his face up close before. He is surprisingly handsome. His jawline is hard and sharpens as he clenches his teeth. He lifts her up, his eyes darting around the room. What is he planning to do with her? She is limp in his arms. He moves at a considerable pace, sprinting outside into the scowling sunlight. It's too bright for her eyes.

"What the fuck, man?" The painter ignores the man outside.

What is he planning? He shifts her weight into one of his arms and shifts the boxes on the back seat of the Golf around with his free hand. She can feel his breath on the back of her neck. Her face is pressed into his chest. He smells of oranges.

"Who is that?" He is careful with her as he puts her down inside the car. "Take her back in. You can't just take her. What the fuck! Do you want Lionel to come after us? I'm not getting into the car until you take her back." How long has he been planning this?

The painter climbs into the driver's seat and starts the car. He begins reversing until eventually the other man chases after him and bangs against the side of the car. The painter pauses for the other man to climb in. The man keeps opening and closing his mouth as though he wants to say something but nothing comes out. Fear is written all over his face.

The car rattles. Her head beats against the window. She catches glimpses of the passing suburbs but her eyes are still too sensitive for her to stare out for long enough to make sense of where she is.

Where is he taking her?

# RUNYARARO
*Life circulates inside*

The roads are busy. His heart feels like it is being controlled by someone else, a foreign arm that has somehow crawled into his body and is holding it, pumping it at a distressing rate. He turns off Acorn Street onto Louis Botha Avenue.

Apart from his heart, everything has stopped. Drivers yell from inside their cars, as though by sounding out their frustration they can make the traffic move. Runyararo curls his hand around the plastic window winder. The window squeals open. Smells of burnt rubber, clutches and exhaust fumes crawl into his nostrils, as he peers outside to try to see what the hold-up is. He can't see any movement up ahead or the cause of the jam. It looks like a badly organized parking lot. He tries to wind the window back up but the glass scrapes against the metal inside the door and doesn't reach the top again.

A woman in a big fancy car to the right of him looks nervously from side to side. She seems aware of Runyararo staring at her. He sees her turn her face forward but her eyes strain toward him. Beady little pupils push as far left as the whites of her eyes will allow.

A whimper comes from the back seat. The girl has started to cry. His heart feels a moment of release. She sounds like a wounded animal.

Shuvai is breathing so hard that he fogs up the passenger window. They are stuck.

What will happen if Lionel figures out that the girl is gone?

He could come after them. Runyararo's chest tightens again. They would be here, unable to move, like easy prey. Who knows what Lionel is capable of? He could have them killed. Someone could be watching them right now. Locked doors don't stop guns. The things we believe keep us safe are useless against a real threat. He inches the car forward.

This is the worst idea he's ever had. When did he decide that he wanted to be brave? He's never been courageous in his life.

A car starts to pull in front of him. They are wedged. The girl lets out a heavy sob from her place behind him. He turns back and sees glutinous bands of snot leaking from her nose. Why did he ever decide to take her? This stupid child isn't worth the risk. He could leave her here. Open the door and let her out. She can figure the rest out for herself. It would be easy. The traffic is hardly moving. He would have enough time to turn off the ignition, open his door, walk to hers and pull her onto the pavement. Her father could come and fetch her.

But if he gets the girl back home, Flora would be astonished.

He would be a hero. The girl would explain his bravery to her entire family. Mr. Joseph might even offer him his job back. He'd be able to see Flora, all day, every day.

Shuvai has been very quiet. Now he lays his head on the dashboard, covering it with his arms as though someone is shooting at him.

Why couldn't he be more like Shuvai? Happy to take what he's offered—just keeps his head down and does the job. No more, no less.

Shuvai is back up and fidgeting. He plays with the buttons on the broken radio. Static noise fills the car. "Does nothing work? Fuck, man!" He turns the radio off.

There's a crash. It resonates through Runyararo's body. The girl sniffs her snot back into her nose and Shuvai sits up straight.

Metal beats against metal. Glass shatters.

Runyararo looks around and sighs with relief as he realizes they were not hit. The woman in the big car opens her door and steps out of her safety zone. She shakes as she moves toward the car she hit. There is no visible damage to her car but the Cressida in front of her has lost its bumper, back lights and rear window. The force of her 4x4 shot the Cressida into the back of a truck. Two men hobble out of the Cressida. They have a few cuts and one is limping badly. At first the woman looks apologetic but within minutes all parties are shouting and pointing out blame.

The girl starts crying again. The line of cars moves forward.

Runyararo watches the accident scene in his side mirror. For someone who looked so vulnerable inside her car, the woman is surprisingly ferocious on the street.

Time is moving faster than they are. They're running late for the delivery. His underarms are clammy. If they don't deliver soon, Lionel will be notified. They can't take the girl with them to the delivery. How would they explain it?

Shuvai is still silent. Why won't he just say something? Usually he talks right up until Runyararo's eyes close at night but now he wants to sit there and shut up.

"Water?" A croak of a voice from the back seat startles him. He turns his head and sees a crack in her lip fill and then release beads of blood. He shakes his head and swivels back to stare at the road.

Her blood is going to mess up the car. What if she dies? They'll blame him. He's the one driving the car with her blood in it. He should stop and get her some water.

Shuvai is huffing and puffing, acting like an infant instead of voicing his frustrations.

The woman and her big car have become small in the mirror but her gestures are big enough to show that the fight is still on.

Their turn-off is two cars away.

# 27

# FARHANA
*It's not all smooth*

"You sure? I can come over and talk to them with you."

"No. It's fine. I just have to do it."

"Well, I can drive over there now. I'll wait in the car, you know if you need to get away after or if you change your mind."

"No, Zee. I can't deal with you and them right now. I'm going to speak to my mum now. I'll text you later."

"Okay. I love you, Farhana." They've said the "love" word before but never like this. It's usually a "love you, babe," more out of habit than a real thought. She never thought that he meant it before.

"Bye." She hangs up abruptly.

The samoosas crackle as her mother lowers them into spurting hot oil. Their coating changes from a pale almost translucent white into golden brown perfection. Her mother scoops them out before they start to burn and lays them on a paper towel to drain off some of the oil.

"Mummy..."

"Yes?" Her mother turns off the stove.

"Do you want some tea?"

"Hmmm. That would be lovely."

Farhana takes the tea and the plate of samoosas to the lounge. It's almost time for the soapies to begin. Her mother watches all of them, starting at half past five, every day. She missed them during Ramsaan. But this week she has received her daily dose with an almost religious fervor.

"Mummy, can we talk?" Her mother turns toward her as the music for *Days of Our Lives* starts to play.

"Yes. What is it?" She can't tell if her mother is impatient because the show is starting or if she's concerned because Farhana has never spoken to her in this tone before. She should have waited until after all the soapies were finished. This is her mother's favorite time of the day.

"Please don't be mad." Farhana stares down at her purple fluffy slippers, more like pillows than slippers. Farhana wants to curl into her mother's lap, escape into the past where this wouldn't be happening.

"What's wrong, bayti?"

"Mummy...I...I'm going to finish my studies..."

"But...Farhana? Have you been failing? I thought that it can't be university holidays for this long." Farhana shakes her head. "Okay, tell me. We can handle it." This is the catchphrase that she and her mother started saying after her father died. Her mother places her hand on Farhana's knee. Her thin wrinkled fingers squeeze through Farhana's tracksuit pants. "Tell me. What's going on?"

Farhana looks at her mother. "I'm pregnant." It shoots out of her mouth. She wants to catch it and put it back inside herself.

Her mother turns off the TV. "What?" Her tone is honest, as though she really didn't hear what Farhana said.

"I'm sorry, Mummy."

"But...how can you? No. Who? How did this happen?"

"Mummy, I...it was a mistake."

"Farhana." Her mother looks up at the ceiling. "I thought you were... we had a plan. Who is the boy?"

"It's Zee. Zilindile, from Eid lunch." Farhana takes a large breath. "He loves me, Mummy."

"What are we going to do, Farhana?" Her mother sits down and starts to undo her bun. She pulls the bobby pins out one at a time. A small mound of black pins slowly grows as her mother's hair loosens into a long thin twist that looks like a koeksister. She unwinds the twist and shakes her head. Her hair falls down to the middle of her back.

Why doesn't her mother say anything? She stares at the blank TV and runs her fingers through her graying hair. When she finally looks at her, Farhana can see tears falling from her mother's face.

"We can handle it, Mummy." Farhana places her hand on her mother's shoulder.

Her mother takes Farhana's hand in hers. She strokes it and then brings it up to her mouth and kisses it. "My baby, we can't handle this one alone. I'm going to call Samad."

# 28

# FLORA

*Coiling in without crossing ways*

"We must be sure that the child is yours. We can't take care of another man's problem. Girls of today, they can do anything. You mustn't just trust." He's too small to have a baby.

"It's mine, Ma. I know it."

"Maybe we must test the baby. I heard they can do that these days. No more lies from easy girls. We can find the truth."

"She's not lying, Ma. If you had spoken to her like a person and not kicked her out onto the street that day, you would know who she is. Do you know how nice her family was to me? They are good people. They invited me in, gave me food..."

"When were you there? Huh? You can't go and negotiate for yourself. There are right ways of doing things, Zilindile."

"Relax, Ma. I was just visiting. That's all. Her mother didn't even know. Farhana is going to tell her today."

"Obviously they were nice to you, then. They didn't know what you did to their daughter. You can be so stupid, Zilindile. Wait until they know, then you will see how nice your Indians are. Only a few days ago you were saying that girl wanted to break up with you, now you are saying she is good."

"Please, Ma. Don't be like this. Leave it alone."

"Leave it! Zilindile, we must go together. We must show them who we are. We don't run from our problems."

There's a knock at the door that makes her jump. She hasn't been able to be calm since the robbery. Why must Mr. Joseph act so strangely when he comes to her room? It's like he's scared to be in her space. Can't he see that all these things were his? Is her room not good enough because it's filled with old stuff? At least she is not wasteful. He stands there with his face pulled like he's been eating a lemon.

If it wasn't for her, his house would be a complete mess. He'll see what it's like if he sells this house. Without her, they won't cope.

"Sorry, Flora. The police are here. I was wondering, when was the last time you saw Cathleen?"

He practically fired her and now she has to come and talk to the police. He already can't manage without her. She told him she was struggling with Zilindile's problems. Mr. Joseph didn't bother to ask why or what was going on. But she must know everything about his children.

He's lucky that she still needs this job. "I don't know, sir. Last week maybe."

She can't actually remember. Can't he keep track of his own children? He didn't even notice that Cathleen was missing in the first place.

"Do you mind coming to talk to them?"

She does mind. This is Mr. Joseph's problem.

Zilindile sits down on the butterfly chair and rests his head in his hands. It's going to be easier to talk to the police than to Zilindile.

She wants to run away. These children are old enough to take care of themselves. When she was Zilindile's age, she had a job and was giving money to her mother, not adding stress to her mother's life.

"Okay, sir."

She closes the door and follows Mr. Joseph into the big house.

# 29

# FRANK
*It's the big toe that balances the foot*

The policemen have made themselves at home. They're relaxing on the couch in front of the empty space where the TV used to be. The fatter one is on Jennifer's side. They are not the same policemen that came previously. Perhaps all the police pairings have a Laurel and Hardy feel to them.

Frank has Cathleen's photograph in his hands. It's the most recent one that he could find but her face has become much more drawn since it was taken. She was happy in this picture. It's from the night of her matric dance. Her hair was shiny and curled into spirals pinned on top of her head. It was the first time Frank had seen her looking like a woman. He didn't want her to go out that night, scared that his baby would disappear. Jennifer had to convince him to let her go with that pimple-faced idiot date of hers. The boy smiled like a cat; Frank didn't trust him.

There was a time when he drove her everywhere. If she came home now, he would do it again. He wouldn't let her leave his side.

What if she's been attacked? When she was scared as a little girl, she would attach herself to his leg until he picked her up. Jennifer said he babied her too much. He should've taught her to defend herself.

"Who was the last person your daughter was with?" Frank shakes his head. "Did you phone her friends? Children of this age are usually at someone else's house."

Frank doesn't know any of Cathleen's friends anymore. He's not sure if she has any.

He looks at Flora. She is standing next to the window, staring out at her room.

He met that girl at the bar, who went to school with Cathleen. What was her name? He could go back and try to find her. But she didn't know that Cathleen had dropped out of university. They seemed to have lost touch.

"Flora?"

"Yes, sir?"

"Do you know any of Cathleen's friends? Does she bring anyone home during the day? Have you seen a car drop her off?"

"No. When she is here, she is always alone."

What is wrong with Flora? It's like she couldn't be bothered to help. What's the point of her being here with the children all day if she's not going to look after them? Doesn't she know anything?

"Where does your daughter go out to?"

"Parties, clubs...I don't know." One of the policemen raises an eyebrow as he makes notes.

It's normal for young people to go out. Cathleen gets frustrated if he asks too many questions. She says she doesn't need an interrogation. He can't keep her captive in the house.

"How does she get around? Does she have a car?"

"She doesn't have a license. There is a second car. Flora's son was teaching her to drive but she lost interest. He drives it at the moment."

The policemen start to talk to Flora in Zulu. Why won't they speak English? Are they discussing his parenting? Are they even talking about Cathleen?

Both policemen stand up and follow Flora into the dining room. He walks to the kitchen and gets himself a glass of water. He really wants a beer. Flora looks at him and moves past him to get two glasses of water for the policemen who are now sitting at the dining room table. No one has sat at the table in ages.

Why is Flora treating them like they're visitors? They're here to do their job.

Frank doesn't know the answers to any of their questions. Flora is as useless. Why doesn't she know? Part of her job is to make sure that the children are taken care of. This is ridiculous.

He stares at Flora and the two policemen. They are talking with smiles on their faces. Do they not realize the severity of the situation? They need to start looking now.

"Flora, where is that phone I gave you to charge?" If the phone belonged to one of Cathleen's friends they might be able to find a clue.

"It's in my room. I forgot to try to charge it. I'll go see now."

She hurries out.

He rests against the wall facing the two officers. The fatter one yawns and stretches, revealing sweat-stained armpits on his uniform. The other one stares blankly at Frank.

"Okay, gentlemen. What's the next step? What do we do now?"

"We'll put the word out, sir. Sounds like a runaway. You will probably find her on your doorstep before we do."

That's it? They're not going to investigate?!

He walks the policemen out and drives to the bar in Parkhurst where he met that girl. Cathleen might be there. He should check all the bars in the area. She could have a boyfriend. Maybe she's been sleeping at her boyfriend's house as some form of rebellion.

The bar looks different now that he's sober. He is the oldest person there. A different group of girls is sitting at the table they were at the last time. They look about Cathleen's age. He walks toward them.

The girl closest to him rolls her eyes as he approaches. "We're not interested buddy, move along." She swings her ponytail over her shoulder and laughs with her friends.

"Sorry, I was just—"

"You're too old for us, okay! We're not interested in sugar daddies." A cackle of laughter erupts from the table.

"I'm looking for my fucking daughter! Her name is Cathleen. Do you know her?"

They're silent. The rest of the tables turn to stare at him. The bartender looks ready to call security. The girl with the ponytail shakes her head.

No. Fuck!

There's a chance that the girl from the other night could still come. He orders a beer and sits at a stool facing the entrance.

# FARHANA
*Dimples consume like quicksand*

Her room is suffocating. The cupboard door can't fully open without banging against the bed. It feels like a prison, her waiting area while her fate is being decided. There is only enough space for her in this room. Where will the baby go if she keeps it? Lying down on the bed, even the ceiling feels like it inches toward her each time she closes her eyes. She types a message to Zee on her phone and then deletes it. What's the point?

The murmured voices of her mother and Uncle Samad filter into the room. But she can't make out what is being said. They're having the family meeting today. She wasn't invited to discuss her life. Along with her mother and uncle, there are two aunts from her mother's side, an uncle she has never seen before and her father's sister.

They've been talking for almost two hours now. She can't walk out into their discussions but she's starting to feel claustrophobic.

There is nothing to do in here.

She should be out there. They haven't spoken to her at all.

She picks up a book. It's a trashy fantasy romance. *Rita watched him step out of the car. His chiseled face and broad shoulders stood out from the crowd. She stared at him, salivating. He was to be her lover. The Voice said that it was her destiny. Now she saw that destiny didn't have...* She rereads the same section over and over but it doesn't sink in. She usually enjoys this type of book when she doesn't want to think. But she can't quiet her mind.

Zee hasn't said what he actually wants. Not that it matters to her family. He's been supportive but completely left the decisions up to her. All he said was that he wants to do right by her. It sounded like a line that belongs in this stupid book. It feels like this isn't real for him. He must have some sort of opinion.

"No! Never!" Her mother is shouting in the lounge.

Farhana decides to tidy her already neat cupboard. She takes out all of her tops and places them on the bed. Many of them won't fit her soon. One by one, she shakes them out and folds them methodically.

A red halter-neck is on top of the pile waiting to be refolded. It's the first present that Zee gave her. It was far more out-there than anything she owned at the time. She only went shopping with her mother so most of her clothes were extremely conservative. When she wore the red halter, she felt like a rebel.

A uniform pile develops in front of her. Next she orders them according to color, then places them back on the shelf in her cupboard. She should rather be ordering them according to what she will be able to wear over her belly. She takes them out again and puts the more revealing ones at the bottom of the pile. But she keeps the halter-neck aside. She won't be able to wear it for a while but she doesn't want it to be forgotten, so she places it between two conservative tops, near the top of the pile.

"Farhana." Her mother is standing at her door. "We are ready for you. Come now."

Following her mother into the lounge feels like going into a court-room. As she enters, they look at her as though she has murdered someone. Uncle Samad is the only one who avoids eye contact. He is looking into his lap as though he's reading a judgment.

Farhana doesn't know where to look. Should she sit down? She doesn't want to sit next to any of them.

"Farhana, what do you think we should do about this?" She didn't expect him to care about what she wants.

"I don't know, Uncle."

"You were acting like an adult, weren't you? Now you must think like one." He is looking directly at her.

"I know that I'm young and that keeping the baby isn't the best option but..."

"That is not an option! You have already shamed us with your be-havior. Now you think that getting rid of the baby is an option?"

She's never heard him shout before. His voice is deep and it feels like the echo remains bouncing back and forth inside her body.

"This is not how you were raised. What would your father think? He is lucky to not be here to see what you have become. Your poor mother, you think she can afford this? Hmm? Throwing away your education like some cheap girl! You know how hard it was for her, on her feet at the shop all day to pay your school fees alone?" His eyes remain on Farhana.

"I want to finish studying. It wasn't for nothing."

"I see. You think you can get everything you want? Who is going to take care of the baby? Your mother? She still has to work. How can you be so stupid? You expect her to take this baby to work?"

"No, I…"

"Enough! You brought enough disgrace on this family with what you did! Disgusting! We won't force you to marry that boy. Why make it any worse? But you must get a job and help your mother pay for things. It's time to take responsibility."

"But, Zee might be…"

"No! That…" He struggles to find his words. "You will have nothing to do with him. You hear me?"

"But…"

"End of discussion."

Her mother has made food for everyone. Farhana excuses herself and goes to her room. She can hear her mother trying to lighten the mood with her terrible joke about the chicken crossing the road and getting curried away. It gets a few forced laughs. How can they all sit there? Her mother didn't say a word the entire time. No one stood up for her.

She goes to the shower. The tiled floor is cold under her bare feet. The water warms her body and drowns out the chatter at the table. She should have allowed Zee to come over. He was going to bring his mother with him. The thought of seeing his mother again was terrifying. Farhana thought that it was best for her to handle her family on her own.

Perhaps Zee could've explained things to them. They need to get to know him. He could help. It wouldn't be much, but he could work until she finishes her studies. Then she could get a decent job. Maybe Zee could study part-time.

What does her uncle expect her to do? Who will hire a pregnant girl without a degree?

She lathers soap onto her facecloth. It's full of bubbles, thick and creamy. The smell of vanilla envelops her.

She could run away. But where would she stay? Zee stays with his mother in a tiny backroom. She won't be able to study if her mother stops paying her fees. She needs to speak to her mother alone. They can't let her uncle dictate what must happen. What has he ever done for them?

She sits down amongst the suds and lets the water fall over her head.

# CATHLEEN

The car stops suddenly.

The painter opens his door and gets out. He pulls her onto the street. They are parked in a cul-de-sac. She can't work out where they are.

He throws her over his shoulder and carries her to an empty field. This is the type of field that always appears in news headlines. Is he planning to rape her? She tries to fight against him, kicking her legs into his stomach but she's too weak to inflict any pain. There's no one around. There's no point in screaming and she doesn't want to risk making him any more angry than he already is.

"Please, I'm sorry. I'll help you...My dad will give you money. I'll do anything."

They are getting further away from the car.

The painter's shoulder pierces into the area just below her diaphragm. When he reaches the grass, his walk has more of a bounce to it. Every step refreshes the pain.

What does he want? What can she offer him?

"My father will understand. I'll tell him that it wasn't you who stole the money. I won't call the police. I won't tell anyone." He puts her down in between some bushes. Branches scratch straight through her skin. He stands over her. Why won't he say anything?

He looks at her and bends down. His hands reach for her skirt. She knew it. If he brings his face close to hers, she will bite. She will bite on any part of him that she can. He pulls her skirt down and covers her underwear before turning and walking away.

What is he doing now? Did Lionel tell him to leave her here? They'll all come, one at a time; first Lionel, then Eddie, and finally the painter.

She hears the car start and drive away from her.

The sun is setting without a hint of a warm glow. Darkness arrives fast. There are creatures crawling over her body. Thin spindly legs tickle as they creep over her. It could be any type of insect. She tries to breathe calmly so as not to disturb them.

After all that has happened she can't believe that she's now scared of being bitten.

She has to get away from here before the men come back. The dry grass cuts at her hands as she pulls her body forward.

# FLORA
*Too far apart*

The phone that Mr. Joseph found is charged and on the kitchen table. She turns it on. It's an old phone, maybe even older than hers. Cathleen would never have a phone like this. Even Zilindile's phone is fancy enough to take photos and play songs. Mr. Joseph doesn't think about these things. How can he believe it belongs to one of Cathleen's friends?

The phone beeps. An envelope sign showing a new message flashes.

Flora nearly drops the phone. The text that she reads is from her.

"Flora." Mr. Joseph is standing behind her. She turns around, holding the phone to her chest. "Is that the phone?" She should shake her head but she nods, pressing the phone into her bosom.

"Well...Did you manage to charge it? Who does it belong to?"

He extends his arm toward her. "Pass it here, let me have a look."

She steps back into the counter.

"No!" She almost screams. Mr. Joseph is confused and starts to come toward her. "It's one of Zilindile's friends." She laughs nervously. "These young boys of today." She signals to the phone. "Too many rude words." She worms her way around Mr. Joseph.

"Goodnight, sir."

It was Runyararo. She can't believe it. The half-painted wall, the way he would smile at her, the flowers and those stolen touches, they were all part of a lie. Runyararo used her to get into the house. She thought he was special.

The SMSs about where she was and when she was coming home all make sense now. It was ridiculous to think that he really liked her. She had actually considered standing up for him when he was fired. All men are after something. If Mr. Joseph had seen the messages, he would have assumed that she was involved in the robbery. She should have believed Cathleen. They should have called the police the first time.

Can Runyararo speak? How much of it was a lie?

Zilindile is sitting on the chair with the butterflies. His eyes are swollen and red. "Farhana phoned. She said she's not allowed to see me anymore."

Flora doesn't want to deal with his problems right now. She can't. How could Runyararo have done this to her? She has been such a fool.

Zilindile's legs are curled up and his feet are on the patterning of the chair. Dirt from his shoes has fallen onto the green fabric. She walks past him and shoves his feet off the chair. He drops his head back, trying to stop the tears from returning.

That stupid girl! How could she have done this to Zilindile?

Flora sits on the armrest next to him and tries to hold him.

His body doesn't soften. He pulls away from her, wrapping his arms around his legs.

She needs some tea. She gets up and puts the kettle on. "Maybe it is better this way, Zilindile. You are off the hook." He doesn't move. "The child is not your problem. If she is so up and down, how can you be sure the baby is yours?"

"It is, Ma."

He will eventually see this as a blessing. She has too much to deal with as it is. When he is older, he can do it all the right way. He can get a job and get married first. She will have to work hard to get him to church every week. Then he will learn to forget and one day he will be able to start afresh.

She takes a cup of tea to him. He is still crying. She places the cup on the floor next to him. She thought that having a son meant she wouldn't have to deal with weeping.

She goes outside to give Zilindile some privacy. A mother shouldn't see her boy in this way. The wall stares at her. It's all there. Runyararo's makeshift seat and table had seemed so wonderful at first. It was like he had a gift of seeing the best in things. Runyararo was definitely clever. He knew what he was doing. At first when he didn't reply to her SMS, she thought he didn't have airtime. Then she worried that he had found someone else. She never thought he was a thief. He got what he needed from her and disappeared. It's the last time that anyone takes advantage of her.

Zilindile must learn not to be a walkover. He must decide what he wants. If he really loves this Farhana, Flora will help him fight for her. Farhana's family can't make all the decisions. If it is her grandchild in that belly, then she is going to fight. She is not going to be taken for a ride again. Both families must make the decision together.

"Zilindile." He hasn't moved but there are no more tears. "It's enough. Get dressed. We are going to see that girl's family."

"They don't want me, Ma. She didn't try for me."

"Enough. We are putting our strong gloves on now. The girl must be struggling also. But today, they will know us!" She goes straight to her cupboard. "Go and wash your face."

"I don't want to start any more trouble for Farhana. Maybe we should give them some time...she's already upset."

"You said it's your baby, nè?" She shakes her head. Zilindile is a good boy. He is the man she should have believed in. He wants to do the right thing.

"Yebo, Mama, but—"

"Fine. Then it's our right to go. They must not think that we are the bad ones here. Go wash your face and then get dressed. And wear proper shoes, no tekkies!"

She must also look presentable. These people mustn't think she's a nobody. This baby must be welcomed.

Her wardrobe is a depressing site. All the nice clothes remind her of Runyararo. She wasted her time and effort dressing up to impress that idiot. She wishes that she owned something that looked professional. Her clothes are either too fancy or too old and broken.

She decides to wear her yellow dress. They must not see that she is disappointed. It is striking and over the top for a visit but they will know that she means business.

"Zilindile! What are you thinking? Take off your jeans and go put on your black pants. This is serious."

Has he lost all his sense? How can he arrive at his future family dressed like a good-for-nothing? No wonder they are concerned about his ability to be a father. At least he has one good pair of black pants. They are a little short and expose too much of his leg when he sits down. But he looks handsome when he is all dressed up like a respectable man.

They get into the Citi Golf and head out. Zilindile is fidgeting with the radio, switching between the stations. The world outside her window changes swiftly. The buildings on the side of the highway look like a painting. Different browns, grays, reds and blues melt into each other.

Mary Fitzgerald Square is full of people. A stage has been set up and someone is performing. She can't make out who it is but the ant-sized people are dancing and enjoying themselves.

Billboards flash past her. There are too many alcohol adverts on this route. It's a wonder that all the people who live in the South are not alcoholics.

The road splits and the old gold mines rise into her view. Massive emptied out sand dunes. There's almost a sparkle to them.

Zilindile drives smoothly. How did he learn to do this so well?

They arrive into the flatness of Lenasia. Flora has never been here before. It's almost like parts of Soweto where big fancy houses are next to their neighbors' tiny homes. Zilindile drives like he knows this route too well. How long has he been seeing Farhana?

They stop opposite a small face-brick house. Flora does not feel ready. Zilindile doesn't get out of the car either. They should drive back home. Her dress suddenly looks too young. Zilindile's leg is trembling. What if there's no one at home? It would have been better to phone first. What was she thinking? Driving up and pushing into someone's house is madness. She knows better.

"You ready, Ma?"

She is not. "Let's go."

They walk slowly along the stone paving toward the wooden front door guarded by a black security gate. What if the family is busy eating?

Zilindile tentatively knocks on the door. A small plump woman opens it. Her pink headscarf makes her look soft.

"Hello Mrs. Bhamjee. This is my mother, Flora."

Flora realizes how strange her name sounds coming out of her son's mouth.

"Hello. Hi, Flora. Please come inside."

They follow Farhana's mother into the lounge. Flora notices how clean the house looks. There are three couches, and a computer in the corner, crowding the small space.

"Please sit down. Farhana! We have visitors."

The girl enters the room. She has obviously been crying like Zilindile.

"Uh...Hello...mam. Hi, Zee." Flora can't stand this Zee business. Can't people at least try to say the name that he was given?

"Farhana, go make some tea."

"Yes, Mummy." The girl leaves the room.

"Flora, I suppose you have come to talk about this situation our children have put us in." Mrs. Bhamjee pulls her scarf further forward.

Flora didn't expect her to be so composed. "Yes, Zilindile, will you excuse us for a few minutes?" He rushes to the kitchen. "You must have been as shocked as I was."

When the mothers are left alone together they start to relax. "I can't tell you all the things that happened in my mind, Flora. We only met your son once before. I had no idea..." She is fighting back tears.

"I was so angry. These children...It's not your fault. They don't listen."

"No. But we had plans for her. It's not the way things were supposed to be. We were almost there. Now...I don't know. We met as a family to discuss it all. I can't afford the baby and the university fees."

"Zilindile can get a good job. I will make sure. We want to...He must help."

"I...I'm sorry, Flora, but it's all feeling too much for me."

"Me too. When I first found out I didn't know what to do. But I knew we had—"

There's a knock at the front door. Mrs. Bhamjee is quick to rise to her feet. "Excuse me, Flora." An elderly man with a large beard, dressed completely in white, appears in the doorway.

"Salaam. This is Flora, Zilindile's mother. Flora, this is Farhana's uncle, Samad."

Flora stands and they shake hands. Then Samad walks to the couch opposite her and sits down.

"Samad, we have been talking about Farhana's...situation."

He leans back into the couch, twirling the end of his beard as he talks. "We have thought about..." Then he sits forward again. "The issue wasn't an easy one to tackle. But we've come to a decision. Farhana will keep the baby but your son will not be a part of her life. It was very good of you to come." He folds his arms, signaling the end of the conversation.

Flora wishes that she could have spoken to Mrs. Bhamjee alone.

Who is this man to tell her what will happen?

Farhana walks into the room with the tea things on a tray.

Zilindile follows close behind with a plate of biscuits. He goes over to greet Samad. They shake hands but Samad avoids Zilindile's eyes. Farhana offers Flora tea. There is a milk jug, sugar and sweetener on the tray. Flora's hands tremble as she pours milk into her cup. Who do these people think they are? She stirs her tea, trying to think of the right words to say while Samad and Mrs. Bhamjee busy themselves with the milk and sugar. Flora takes a sip of her tea and stands up.

"We also talked as a family. We have decided that it is best for them to get married. My son will be a good father."

Zilindile opens his mouth as if to say something. What a nerve!

Flora gives him a piercing look. The adults are talking. He knows better than to interrupt.

Samad blows on his tea before he speaks. "I'm afraid the decision has been made. What can you and your son give this baby?"

Flora feels silly standing in front of this big-headed man.

Zilindile turns away. "This baby is his! It is my grandchild. We have the right—"

"Yours? This idiot made this mess and now you want rights! I don't think you've thought this through. It's better if you go now. No need to fight." He turns to Mrs. Bhamjee. "Open for them."

She stands and picks up the keys as she's instructed. Zilindile follows her out. Farhana is staring at Zilindile; she starts to cry as he steps out the door. Flora knows that look. Farhana is in love with her son.

Flora steps toward Samad, pulling her shoulders back. "You be careful of what you say." He stands up. Flora can feel his breath. It's moist from the tea. She has to crane her neck back to look into his eyes. "My son is no idiot. He wants to take responsibility. You should be happy. Did you ask Farhana what she wants?"

"We don't ask children questions they can't answer." Samad brushes past Flora as he walks to the door where Mrs. Bhamjee is standing.

What is wrong with this mother? Does she not have a mouth of her own? This is the problem with women! This is why men feel like they can take what they want. It is women like Mrs. Bhamjee, allowing men to have all the say.

"Don't worry, my boy, we won't stop fighting."

# RUNYARARO
*Struggling to push past the bars*

He is grateful for the warmer weather. Leaving Cathleen in the winter cold would have been the same as killing her. The darkness is overwhelming.

Where is she? He looks back at the car. This seems like the right distance but everything is different without the sunlight. He gets down on his hands and knees. He should have brought a torch.

The grass is wet. What if she managed to leave? She couldn't have made it home by now. She seemed petrified when he left her here.

If only he could have reassured her and told her that he would be back. This veld is littered with broken glass, cigarette stubs and all sorts of unidentifiable unsanitary objects. He is slow to place his hand down, hoping to find the warmth of her body. Sticks and rocks meet his hands, scratching away at the skin on his palms. His landmarks for finding her again have disappeared with the light. She was too weak to survive an entire night here.

What if someone else found her? She could have been raped and killed. Why didn't he think of that? They had to rush to deliver the boxes. Something mushy oozes underneath his right hand. He tries to wipe it off on the wet grass.

What is Flora going to say? He has failed.

# CATHLEEN
### Need to be trimmed

Purple flowers form a carpet along her street. She's finally home. It's hard to believe that she's made it. The jacarandas provide cushioning under her torn black fingernails. Her body wants to collapse and surrender into the sweet smelling flowers. A soft wind spirals another downpour of flowers that start to cover her body. She could stay here until morning. It would be a better night's sleep than she's had in a while. The flowers underneath her soften into a sticky mess. She pulls herself forward and rests on fresh flooring. Flowers attach themselves to her hair and face.

Her house is in sight.

She lifts herself up at the gate and rests against the bell.

What if no one is home? She lies down on a patch of grass in front of the gate. Lionel has her address. It might be better to stay outside. What has happened at the house? Her entire family could have been killed.

Headlights blind her. A car pulls into the driveway. It's a small car. She can't make out the specifics through the lights but the shape looks like a Golf. They've come to get her. It was stupid to come back home. The painter knows this house. Why didn't she think about that? She gets up and tries to run but slips on the jacaranda petals. Two people get out of the car. She has nothing left to give them. She gets up again. Hands grab her purple-lined arms. She screams. The hands firmly turn her around. Her face falls into a soft small bosom. Thin arms stop her from wriggling. The smell of childhood creeps into her. It's a combination of flour, tea, fabric softener, lotion and hair oils—the smell of home. Cathleen releases into Flora's body. Flora and Zee carry her into the house.

The bath water is warm. The petals float to the surface as Cathleen's body soaks. Flora takes a facecloth, wets it and gently wipes away the residue left from the flowers. She gets a plastic jug and fills it with water. Cathleen knows this routine from when she was a little girl. Flora tells her to tilt her head back and pours the water onto Cathleen's hair.

Her hand creates a barrier at the top of Cathleen's forehead to prevent water from falling into her eyes, while humming an incomplete melody. As a child, Cathleen used to swing her wet hair around. Flora struggled to get out of the way but was always a little wet after bath time.

Flora turns Cathleen's body around and starts to shampoo her hair. Cathleen remembers Dina spraying her with cold water from the showerhead. She starts to cry. Flora continues to wash her hair.

Her bedroom hasn't changed. It's much neater than when she was last home but the walls are still plastered with familiar magazine cutouts and random quotes. Red letters above her mirror state: *We are, because we said so.* She used to think the quote was so deep. It was a tag line for a jeans advert. What does it even mean?

She sits up and sees her reflection in the mirror. She's clean now and a bit shiny from the Vaseline Flora smeared on her face. Her hair is still damp and plaited into a thin line down her back. Cathleen used to love this hairstyle. She would beg Flora to plait her hair before suppertime. Then she would sway down the stairs feeling like a princess.

The door opens. Flora comes in with tea and toast and sits down on the side of the bed. Cathleen takes the tea. It is hot but she has a long swallow. It is sugary and delicious. The warmth spreads through her body. Flora watches her take a bite of the buttered toast. Cathleen is exhausted. Flora moves the plate and cup and covers her with her duvet before leaving the room. She lets a crack of light in through the open door.

# 35

# FLORA
*To be read by a fortune-teller*

She couldn't believe her eyes and didn't want to know the answers to all the questions running through her mind. Cathleen was wet, a brown mush coated her frail body and bones jutted out at awkward angles. What had happened to her? It was like when the madam got really sick, her skin became pale and thin, almost see-through. The house went quiet like it is now. Flora did her best to look after the madam. There was nothing that could be done. Mrs. Joseph became like a child. Flora prayed at her bedside every day. At first she prayed for the madam to get better but at the end she prayed for her soul to be taken. It was too terrible for the children to see their mother like that.

Flora couldn't watch it happening again. She didn't want to sit in the room with Cathleen while she ate those small difficult bites. It's like Cathleen's mouth couldn't open any wider. She hasn't said anything about what happened to her but randomly bursts into tears, letting Flora know that whatever it was it's not forgotten.

Flora is holding the fort outside Cathleen's room like a security guard. The washing can wait. She stands there and stares at the beige passage wall, hoping to hear life re-enter Cathleen's body.

No one ever fought with Flora the way that Cathleen did. She was always a clever girl but after the madam died the fights got very bad. Flora never thought she would miss their fights. She so often wanted to give up on Cathleen but she had taken care of her since she was a little girl.

Mr. Joseph has been useless. He comes out of his bedroom and stares at Flora. "So, how is she?" He was the same with his wife.

Last night, he didn't even help to carry Cathleen up the stairs. He just kept stepping from side to side, as if there were hot coals under his feet. Then he went downstairs. He still hasn't spoken to her.

Flora doesn't answer his question and simply nods toward her bedroom. He sighs and goes downstairs. Flora walks back into Cathleen's room. She has fallen asleep. Flora rearranges the covers on the bed and takes the dishes downstairs.

Mr. Joseph has gone out. How can he think about doing anything else when his daughter is like this?

Flora pours some cold water into a glass and takes it up to Cathleen's room. She sits at the desk and listens to Cathleen's soft breathing. The inhale is deep and is followed by a long almost purposeful exhale. The repetitive breathing is calming and Flora finds herself breathing in time with Cathleen.

The garden is wild and overgrown. Flora can see the whole backyard from the window. Her room is tiny compared to the garden. Mr. Joseph is back. He is walking with an older lady who has a clipboard in her right hand. She doesn't look impressed with the state of the garden. They are closely followed by a couple who are holding hands as they inspect the garden. The couple are full of smiles as they stare up at the house. Flora stares back.

They must see that this home is lived in. The man waves at her and says something to his wife. Flora sits back, out of their view.

These people have some nerve waving at her. Why would Mr. Joseph bring people here when his daughter is sick in bed? He can't come in and speak to Cathleen but there he is chatting away with strangers.

She peeps out of the window again. Mr. Joseph has opened her room door. They are all walking inside. Her room is upside down. If he had told her before, she could have tidied things up.

He has no right to go in there without asking.

They are back outside in less than five minutes. Was her room not interesting enough for them? If they know what's good for them, they won't try to talk to her. She will tell them what is what. They are headed toward the big house. She gets up and locks Cathleen's door from the inside.

She hears them coming up the stairs and stands back and glares at the wooden door. Their laughter is unnatural and feels forced. Mr. Joseph must be trying to tell them one of his jokes that no one understands. The laughter lets her know which room they are in. They are getting closer. She should tidy up around Cathleen. She straightens out the duvet. Cathleen looks like she's advertising the most comfortable bed in the world and doesn't stir at all while Flora is faffing around her. Someone pushes down on the door handle. It doesn't budge. Nervous giggles slide under the door. They knock lightly. Flora doesn't move. Another knock. It's more insistent than the first. Flora folds her arms and stares at the door. Cathleen is fast asleep.

"Hello?" Mr. Joseph's voice breaks in his effort to sound cheerful.

"Flora...Could you let us in please? These people have come to look at the house." He is trying to use his most polite tone. This isn't the time to show the house. She turns her back on the door and walks to the window.

How can he let these people see his daughter like this? Can't he wait with selling it? "Flora!" He growls. Where will they go?

Cathleen needs her. The people with him start whispering amongst themselves. He pushes against the door. Flora hasn't had the time to look for a job. The hinges of the door are straining to hold on. Zilindile is about to become a father, she needs an income.

Cathleen turns over, disrupting the neatened bedding. Who is going to hire her? "You better open this door!" He starts banging his weight against it repeatedly. Cathleen wakes up and starts crying without realizing what's happening. Cathleen sees her father fall into her room.

Her voice is small but clear. "Dad, you came for me."

The other people have already gone downstairs.

# 36

# FARHANA
*Always space for more*

This is the only bedroom she can remember staying in. Her father bought her the bed ten years ago. Her first big girl bed. She went with him to the shop to buy it. It was the day she turned twelve.

She was starting high school the following year. There was so much to be excited about but the drive to the shop felt serious. Her father's forehead was creased like a crumpled newspaper. His voice was full of concern as he spoke about the next phase of her life.

"Things are about to change in ways that may sometimes confuse you." His voice was clear as he stared at the road ahead.

"Your mother and I are proud of you but you are no longer a little girl. It's time to take life into your own hands. We will be here but we can only lead you so far. Your studies must now become your priority. You can have a good life one day. If you work hard, everything will fall into place. Too many young girls get distracted when they become women; they focus only on socializing. Don't worry about this. There will be plenty of time in the future." He smiled at her, revealing the dimples he had given her. She nodded back at him. It had seemed so simple at the time.

Following him into the bed shop, she realized how short her dad was. The top of her head was in line with the hairs on the back of his neck. He smiled at one of the shop assistants. "We are looking for a nice double bed for my big daughter." They looked at all the beds in the shop. Falling onto mattresses to see which was the most comfortable. The decision was entirely hers.

On the drive home, her father spoke to her like she was an adult. He asked her questions about her life and what she wanted to be. She wasn't certain about any of her answers and sometimes changed her mind mid-sentence but he listened to all the possibilities she dreamed about. Nothing was beyond reach.

The bed doesn't look as big anymore but the room seems very small. She lifts her suitcase and her tog bag onto the bed. It doesn't take long to pack because her cupboards are so well organized.

All her panties, socks and bras go into the small bag. The rest go into her suitcase. She packs enough clothes to last two weeks: a few loose dresses, two jerseys, her favorite pair of jeans, some tracksuit pants and a mixture of fancy tops and T-shirts. Only three pairs of shoes will fit into the suitcase with the clothes. Her toiletries go into the tog bag with her underwear. She closes the bags and goes to check on her mother.

She stands looking at her mother's bedroom door for a few minutes. Her mother is going to be all alone. Farhana peers in from the passage. Her body rises and falls under the heavy duvet. There is absolute calm in her face as though she has released all of her worries. After her father died, Farhana used to crawl into her mother's bed. His smell lingered in the room for months. Her mother would throw her arm around Farhana and pull her into a tight cuddle. She wouldn't let go until morning. What will her mother do when she wakes up? Would things have been different if her father was alive?

Three hoots announce Zee's arrival at the house. Farhana wants to go in and kiss her mother goodbye but the risk of waking her is too high. She pulls the bedroom door closed.

Zee is standing outside. The boot of the car is open. He hurries over to help her carry the bags. Farhana's fingers tremble as she slides her house keys through an open window. They are her goodbye note.

This could be a huge mistake. Zee squeezes her hand and walks her to the car. Lenasia is different tonight. The narrow streets and familiar houses are badly lit by the glimmer of the crescent moon. As they turn the corner, all the lights are out. The entire neighborhood is in complete darkness. Her mother will wonder when the blackout started. She'll go through the freezer and check that all the food is fine. Farhana won't be there to help her reorganize. Maybe she should stay one more night. She looks at Zee. He smiles and kisses her gently.

She rolls her window down. They are driving on the highway.

Lenasia is now a twinkle of lights in the rear-view mirror. Will she ever go back? The wind whips in through the open window and tosses her hair around. He strokes her thigh. Her jaw is tight as she speaks to him. "What are we going to do? Have you thought about this?" she shouts above the wind. She's angry. It's not about him but she can't stop herself. "You're taking this so lightly. It's not a joke, Zee."

He glares at her. "What more do you want from me? I'm here. And we made this decision together. You said this is what you wanted." His words are flung about by the wind. She closes the window.

"I know. I'm just stressed..."

"I promise to make things better. We have to stay with my mother, until I can figure something out. It won't be for long."

# RUNYARARO
*Squeezing forward*

The words are starting to surface. He's trying not to swallow. He doesn't want to wash them away. They are necessary. He is pacing the stretch of pavement in front of the house. He knows he looks suspicious but he needs the time to build the words. Consonants bounce between his teeth and his throat while the vowels stir his stomach into knots.

What will he do if Mr. Joseph answers the bell? He needs Flora's face to give the sounds meaning. If she could come outside he'll be able to work out how to explain everything. It would be much easier if he had his phone. He should have borrowed Shuvai's phone. How is he going to tell her? If she holds onto his hands, sentences will pour out of him. He needs to break the silence.

But if he tells Flora about Cathleen, he will have to tell her everything. Chaos will crawl from his mouth and destroy her. She won't understand. She will extract her hands from his. He should just go home and come back once it's all forgotten.

But Cathleen could die out there. He needs to tell someone.

Flora might be so surprised to hear his voice that she won't think about all that he's done. When they find Cathleen, Flora will forgive him.

He rings the doorbell. James, the little boy, answers on the intercom.

"Hello." Runyararo gulps, sweeping his words back down into his belly. He stares at the speaker, willing the words to climb back up to his mouth.

The boy repeats himself. "Hello?"

Runyararo can't reply. This isn't going to work. He presses the bell again.

James answers again, "Hellooo."

Runyararo taps on the speaker with his finger. Where is Flora?

He can't speak without her.

"Who's there, James?" It's Mr. Joseph's voice.

"I don't know. Must be some stupid kids. No one is saying anything."

Runyararo rings the bell again. This time he keeps his finger firmly pressed down on the buzzer. Eventually the big man comes outside.

Mr. Joseph takes a step back when he sees Runyararo. "What in hell's name are you doing here?"

This is too difficult. Runyararo wants to disappear like his ability to speak.

"Hmm? Do you want me to call the cops?"

Runyararo stands up straight and shakes his head.

Mr. Joseph waves his hand at him. "Then get lost. Do you know what time it is?"

Runyararo nods.

"Oh! You do. Well, then did you just come here to stare at me at this time of night?"

Runyararo needs to think of something. He kneels down on the pavement.

"For God's sake! Come on, man. Get up. You're not getting your job back. Stand up." Mr. Joseph looks more and more agitated.

Runyararo's fingers move swiftly on the ground.

"Please, I'm selling the house. There is no job anymore. It's done."

Runyararo stands up and points to the ground. Small stones spell out *FLORA*.

"Flora! What? Is that what this is all about?" Mr. Joseph is red in the face and yells at the top of his voice: "Floooraaahh!"

# 38

# FLORA
*Who knows no truths*

Mr. Joseph has gone completely insane. He hasn't stopped shouting since he flew through Cathleen's bedroom door. One look at his daughter's face and the next thing he was pulling Flora out of the room, threatening her.

What does he want now? It took her forever to calm Cathleen down. She tried singing to Cathleen, holding her, rocking her and making her tea but nothing worked. Flora was exhausted.

Cathleen cried for hours.

At first it was a quiet sob, a few gasps to assist with her quickened breathing, but then it grew into a howl, hard and piercing, before returning back to the softer weeping. Flora thought it was never going to end. Eventually she took Cathleen downstairs to sit on the couch with James. Cathleen seemed to make an effort to collect herself in front of her brother.

Flora still hasn't had the chance to check on Zilindile. He sped out of the yard an hour ago. Now this stupid man has started his yelling all over again. Flora can see that both Cathleen and James are growing more and more anxious as their father keeps shouting. She feels like giving him a good klap. He's already fired her. What more can he do? She doesn't deserve this kind of treatment.

She finds him at the gate. "Sir?"

"It seems you have a visitor."

Her body turns cold when she sees him standing in the road.

"Thank you, sir. I will deal with it." Mr. Joseph storms back into the house.

"What are you doing here?" she hisses at him. "Did you come for your phone?"

Runyararo shakes his head.

Flora wants to scream, she wants to embarrass him and expose him for what he really is but she doesn't want to upset Cathleen, so she whispers as viciously as she can. "You are disgusting. You think I don't know what you were doing with me? I'm not an idiot. Just get lost."

He stares at her.

"Are you stupid? Voetsek man!"

Runyararo kneels down in front of her. She wants to kick him. He starts doing something on the ground. "Go! Just get out of here. I know everything. Do you want me to call the police? I'll tell them you were the one who robbed the house!"

"Flora?" Cathleen is standing next to her. Mr. Joseph is standing behind his daughter. Cathleen starts trembling, her face is pale and it looks as though she might faint. "It was him."

She starts shrieking. Mr. Joseph disappears back into the house.

Tears run down Cathleen's face. "He took me."

Mr. Joseph is back and pushes past Flora. He has a cricket bat in his hand. Runyararo is still kneeling on the ground. Cathleen's crying is like a siren disturbing the silence of the neighborhood. James is at the gate, he tries to calm his sister but the more he tries to hold her, the louder she gets.

Mr. Joseph steps forward, the bat held firmly in his hands. He swings the bat through the air. Cathleen swallows her sound and for a moment there is perfect silence. Runyararo looks up at Flora, his eyes begging her to intervene. James and Cathleen turn away. The bat comes down and connects cleanly with Runyararo's head. It sounds like the earth coming apart. A deep guttural sound escapes from his mouth. It's the only sound that Flora has ever heard from him. Runyararo's head hits the pavement, his body collapsing onto the street.

Silence returns.

# 39

# FARHANA
*This space is taken*

Sirens drown out the music playing on the car radio. Flashing lights brighten the whole street. There are police cars and people all around the property. She thinks she sees a body being put in the back of an ambulance. What's happened here?

Zee swerves the car onto the curb, gets out and races toward the house. She tries to follow him but can't keep up. He disappears into the crowd. Farhana squeezes through a group of policemen.

They are standing around a dark brown puddle on the pavement, next to some stones that look like they're trying to spell something out. Farhana thinks she can make out WE HAVE TO FIND. A stained cricket bat finishes the sentence.

No one stops her from entering the house. She has never gone in from the front door before. The painting at the bottom of the stairs of the woman with the blurred features is the first thing she sees.

A large man is standing in the corner next to a window talking to some policemen. She still can't find Zee. There's a girl sitting on the couch. It's Cathleen. Is this Cathleen's house? Is that who Flora works for?

Cathleen notices her. Farhana sits down next to Cathleen.

"Hey Cath, haven't seen you in ages." She wants to tell Cathleen about the baby, Cathleen won't judge her. "It's been crazy, Zee and I—"

Cathleen starts to cry.

"What's wrong? What happened, Cath?" Farhana strokes Cathleen's arm, it's thin and coarse.

The large man walks toward them. He must be Cathleen's father. Farhana gets up and makes space for him on the couch. He puts his arm around Cathleen, pulling her into his chest.

"It's all going to be fine. Don't worry. I'm going to take you away from all of this. We're going to stay with your grandparents in Cape Town. I got a job there. We need to just forget about all this and start anew."

Farhana goes to find Zee. Does he know that Cath is leaving?

Where are they going to stay? She finds him in the backroom, on the floor stuffing clothes into a suitcase.

"What's going on?" The room is tiny. It's about the size of her mother's lounge.

She sees the mattress on the floor, next to the single bed. Is that where they were going to sleep? What was she thinking? How could the three of them stay here? Why is he packing?

"Farhana, I can't explain now. Can you just start getting the kitchen things together?" His voice is tired.

"Together for what, Zee?"

"I said that I'll tell you later!" He's never spoken to her in such a harsh tone before.

She finds a cardboard box under the sink. Where is Zee's mother? She opens the cupboard. There are four plates, two bowls, three glasses and a few mugs. She puts the crockery into the box that is too big for the handful of items, which rattle around. If she calls her uncle now, things will only get worse. It might not be too late to speak to her mother.

Zee comes up behind her and strokes her belly as he hands her some newspaper. She takes the crockery back out of the box and individually wraps each item in newspaper before placing them back in the box. She puts the dishcloths, tea, sugar and the cutlery on top of the crockery. Zee takes the box from her and carries it outside, along with the suitcase he was packing.

Flora takes measured steps into the room, moving as though each step is a deliberate decision. There are splatters of blood on her clothes. She sits down on the green chair.

She sighs and rubs her hand across her forehead as she notices Farhana. "It is better for you to go home now. I know what I said but I can't. We can't help you. Please, it will be better if you go."

Farhana walks outside. She sits down and stares into the main house through the large windows. It's still chaotic in there. Zee is sitting next to Cathleen on the couch. They are talking and Zee is stroking Cathleen's face. Zee doesn't care about Farhana. Would they have stayed together if she wasn't pregnant?

She stands up and walks through the house to the front door. Zee doesn't seem to notice her. He is whispering to Cathleen, whose head is now on his lap. Farhana knew that something was going on between the two of them. She should have trusted herself. She should have trusted her family; they made the right decision for her. Zee must take her home. He brought her here. This is not what he promised. It's his responsibility to take her back. She might be able to reach the key through the window.

No one will have to know what happened tonight.

She walks to the couch. "Zee."

He continues to rub Cathleen's head as he looks up at Farhana. "What?"

"I changed my mind. I want to go home."

"Do you not see what's happening here? Fuck, man! This isn't about you."

# FRANK
*Keeping it leveled*

There are boxes all over the place. When did they accumulate so many things? He thought that after the robbery it would be easier to pack, but it feels like the thieves didn't make a dent. He can't work out what to take and what to leave. Cathleen and James are busy packing up their rooms. It feels too abrupt. He hasn't got a buyer yet. But he can't live with Jennifer's ghost any longer. After the robbery and what happened to Cathleen, he doesn't even want to be in Johannesburg anymore.

Jennifer's side of the cupboard is still untouched. She would want her clothes to be given away. He takes her dresses, skirts and shirts and piles them into boxes as quickly as he can. But her smell finds him—a light fruity fragrance drifts off the clothes and onto him. He can't contain it in a box. A long green silk dress sits on top of the pile of clothes. The last time she wore it, they were away on holiday. She was saving it for when she got better, when she could go out to dinners and events where that sort of dress was appropriate.

He could put her things in storage.

"Dad?" Cathleen is standing in the doorway. He hasn't been able to talk to her properly since she disappeared. He can't bear to know what she went through. He has failed her. He was supposed to protect her and each time she tries to speak to him he feels terrified that she might tell him something that he won't be able to live with, so he tries to avoid the conversation.

"Yes." He keeps packing. He can't bring himself to look at her.

"I think I made a mistake."

If he allows her to continue, she might never stop.

He used to crave the sort of relationship where his children would tell him everything but now that sounds like a curse. He did what needed to be done in the end. He stood up for his daughter.

When the bat hit the painter's head, Frank could feel the vibrations through the handle. They took the painter to Johannesburg General Hospital. He's in a coma. The police didn't interrogate Frank. They believed what he had to say. The painter was another nameless criminal, taken away. They said they will only be able to charge the painter when or if he wakes up. What will happen if he dies? Will Frank be charged with murder? He doesn't want to hear about any mistakes.

"Do you want any of your mother's clothes? They're in those boxes."

He moves past her and goes downstairs. He'll send her to therapy when they're settled in Cape Town.

Jennifer would have been able to talk about the difficult things.

He's grateful that Cathleen doesn't follow him.

The paintings were all chosen by Jennifer. He should sell them.

He takes a large oil painting of a blurred woman's face off the wall.

He has never understood art. For her fortieth birthday he bought her a sketch of two people dancing. He thought it was the type of art that she loved—simple and romantic. She said it lacked meaning. He sold it when she got sick and found out that it really wasn't worth what he'd paid for it. They'll probably get more money from selling the ones that Jennifer bought. It'll be a month before his new job starts paying and they'll need to find a place to live soon. It will be strange to create a home with only the three of them.

# 41

# RUNYARARO
*Soldered in place*

Starched linen holds him securely. There is a small hole in the sheet, near his big toe. He forces his toe through the hole. It gets stuck for a minute before he can pull it out again. There are five other beds in the room. High-rise beds on wheels, like trolleys, easy to move. Nameless, faceless people have been by his side.

How long has it been? The man next to him is screaming. He remembers the scream from his dreams. It was Flora screaming in his dreams. Her mouth was spread wide like the ocean, torrents of pain gushing out of her and into him. His head is tensing in time with the beeping of one of the machines in the room.

He hears footsteps approaching and closes his eyes. A sharp needle pricks into his skin. He tries to keep his muscles still. The vein is missed. The needle tries again, this time with success. Blood is drawn from his body. The man next to him is still screaming but the person with the needle seems unconcerned and leaves the room.

It is never quiet in this place.

The lights are always on.

Trousers are forced onto his body by rough calloused fingers. He is pulled into a seated position. Shuvai lifts him off the bed.

"We have to go, man. They're starting to ask questions about your name and where we live." The screaming starts again. It turns into the continuous hooting of cars. His head bounces against the taxi's window.

Shuvai helps him out of the taxi. How are they going to make it up all those stairs? Shuvai should leave him on the street. There's nothing left for him. Flora's face said it all. Did Lionel find out about the girl? He'll be looking for them. Shuvai needs to find a new place to live. They need to disappear. Shuvai puts Runyararo on his back. Runyararo's arms dangle around Shuvai like a necklace. Shuvai holds onto Runyararo's hands as he starts the journey up the stairs.

A drone of pain whirls around Runyararo's head. Where is Flora? Could she have forgiven him? Perhaps the girl finally explained that he was trying to help? Or maybe Shuvai explained it. Flora might be sitting at the top of the stairs, her slender fingers wrapped around the handle of a mug as she sips some tea.

Shuvai is breathing heavily when they reach the eighth floor.

He holds Runyararo up with one arm as he opens the black gate and swings the door open.

There are only blank walls waiting to welcome him.

"I've got to get to work. Lionel said I have to be there on time. I told him that a car hit you. Your share of the money is next to the mattress.

"Look, man, I reckon you should take it and go back home."

# 42

# CATHLEEN

*Wigs aren't real*

Girls with sun-bleached blonde hair, tanned legs and microskirts walk past the queue waiting to enter the club. They kiss the enormous mustached bouncer on the cheek and slink under the red corduroy rope that separates the in crowd from the rest. Cathleen struggles to control her heels on the cobblestone walkway.

An anorexic wannabe-model sits on a high red stool with a guest list and a power high. She denies a group of men entry because they don't have the right shoes on.

Cathleen steps forward, ready for scrutiny.

The girl looks Cathleen up and down. "It's a hundred rand."

Cathleen hands the money over and the red rope is released.

The world inside is sad and obvious. Chandeliers hang from the steel ceiling, providing low enough lighting to disguise the cheap flooring. Commercial house music blares through the speakers. She's too sober to survive here. All the girls look the same and all the guys are manicured. All at ease in this home of theirs.

They look at her. She doesn't belong. She's an intruder who has managed to slip past the secured fortress and into their secret lair.

She heads to the long black bar. There are three barmen spinning bottles as if they're auditioning for a movie. Finally, a dark-haired, green-eyed barman comes over to her.

"What's your poison?" His smile is too flashy.

"Double vodka and a shot of tequila on the side." She turns around to face the room. No one is interested in her.

"Anything else?" There's a twinkle in his eye that she's familiar with.

"What would you suggest?" She's not used to this crowd. It's awkward. She has no connections in this stupid city.

"Speak to my man over there, the one in the blue shirt. His name is Joe."

Joe is standing in the corner on the opposite side and seems to know everyone here. The fastest way to get to him is to walk straight across the dance floor, through the cavernous space that's empty because they're all still too sober to dance.

She downs her tequila. It doesn't give her enough bravery. She takes the long way round, keeping close to the edges to avoid the eyes in the room. A few of the cloned girls along the walls giggle as she passes them.

Joe is taller than his slouched posture suggests. He has ginger hair and freshly-sprouting stubble on his chin. He's not as well built as the average guy in here. A small but firm paunch pushes against the buttons of his shirt. She smiles at him.

He looks at her out of the corner of his eye.

"Ja?"

"Er...the bartender, the one with the green eyes, he said you might have something for me." This is ridiculous. She feels retarded. Why is she acting like this is the first time she's tried to buy?

"Three hundred."

She misses Zee. She hands over the money.

He drops a little bag into her purse. It better be good stuff.

She heads to the toilets.

# 43

# FLORA
*Short nails struggle to scratch*

The plastic seats are all occupied. A few people stand with their backs against the wall. The woman standing next to Flora is barefoot, exposing the bulging swell of her feet. How can skin stretch that much? The woman's ankles disappear into her balloon feet. They are like hooves being lifted off the ground one at a time, showing the black dirt stains on the soles of her feet. Flora looks up at the woman, who is wiping her face with a dishcloth. She is such a large woman, it's impossible to tell if she is pregnant or not. Flora's phone beeps. It's another message from Runyararo. She turns the phone on silent and puts it into her bag.

Zilindile and Farhana are making their way back toward her, squeezing through the crowded waiting room. They are both so small but their faces have aged over the last few months. Farhana clutches her round stomach as she sidles past people.

"Our name is on the list, Ma. They said we must wait until they call us." Zilindile sighs through his words. His voice has become softer, like he's too tired to talk anymore. He slides down against the wall behind Flora and sits on the floor.

Farhana stands next to Flora. Will she ever tell her mother that she is still with Zee? The two women stare straight ahead.

A man walks toward them. He is out of breath and emits the smell of old sweat. Farhana lifts her scarf to cover her nose.

In an effort to get to the swollen-footed woman, the man bumps Flora into Farhana, who opens her arms to catch Flora and they momentarily waddle about in an awkward embrace, stumbling this way and that, knocking into other patients as they struggle to regain balance.

"Hey watch it." Zilindile jumps up and steadies them.

Flora looks at Farhana, her lips are tightly pursed.

"What is wrong with the two of you?"

Flora and Farhana burst out laughing. People turn to look at them, shaking their heads. Laughing is bad manners in a clinic.

The scowling nurse at the front desk finally calls them.

Farhana looks at Zilindile and then at Flora. "Zee, do you want to ask your mother to come inside with us?"

Flora nods and follows them. Maybe they have that machine that shows you the baby. She's happy not to miss the first picture of her grandchild.

# GLOSSARY

**Atchar** .............A pickle or spicy condiment, often eaten with curry.

**Azaan** ..............The Islamic call to prayer.

**Bayti** ...............Daughter.

**Breyani** ...........An Indian rice dish.

**Burfi** ................An Indian sweetmeat.

**Chana Magaj** ...An Indian sweetmeat.

**Dal** ..................Cooked lentils.

**Doek** ...............A piece of cloth worn wrapped around the head
by African women.

**Dua** .................A prayer/calling out to God.

**Eid** ..................Festival/Holiday. In this case it refers to Eid
al-Fitr, the feast of breaking the fast.

**e.tv** .................The first and only privately owned free-to-air television
station in South Africa.

**Faff** .................To spend your time doing things that aren't
very important.

**Gee** .................Urdu word for "yes."

**Ghee** ...............Clarified butter.

**Iftar** ................A meal eaten after sunset during Ramsaan.

**Jalebi** ..............An Indian sweetmeat.

**Klap** ................To hit *(Afrikaans)*.

**Koeksister** .......A traditional South African donut that is sticky and sweet.

**Matric** .............To matriculate is to graduate from secondary school.
"Matric" is often used to reference the exams high
school students take in order to graduate. To "have"
matric is to have graduated. "After matric" is after
graduation.

**Molana** ...........A respected Islamic scholar/leader.

**Mubarak** .........Blessed. Eid Mubarak is a greeting used on the Eid festivals.

**Oros man** ........Oros is a juice-flavored drink common in South Africa. The Oros man is an orange mascot, a round man with a big belly, who advertises Oros.

**Provitas** ...........A wholewheat cracker popular in South Africa.

**Punjabi** ...........A type of Shalwar kameez, where the top is cut straight with side slits and the pants are wide at the top but tight and gathered at the ankle.

**Qur'an** ............The Islamic sacred book.

**Ramsaan** .........The ninth month in the Islamic calendar. Muslims fast from sunrise to sunset during during this holy month.

**Roti** .................An Indian bread.

**Salaam** ............A greeting signifying peace, used chiefly by Muslims.

**Samoosa** .........Samosas, an Indian fried pastry with savory fillings.

**Sehri** ...............The meal consumed before sunrise during the fasting month.

**Shebeen** .........An informal drinking establishment.

**Sisi** .................Sister.

**Spaza** ..............A small shop on the side of the road or in urban townships selling chips, chocolates, cigarettes and other small items.

**Stoep** ..............A terraced porch in front of a house *(Afrikaans).*

**Tekkies** ...........Sneakers.

**Topi** ................An Islamic prayer hat, generally a skull cap.

**Tsotsi/Tsotsis** ..Gangster/gangsters.

**Veld** ................Field (Afrikaans).

**Voetsek** ..........Get lost! Go away! *(Afrikaans).*

**Yebo** ...............Yes *(Zulu).*

# ACKNOWLEDGEMENTS

This book would not have been possible without the love and support of my parents, Mohamed Patel and Yasmin Adam, and my siblings, Inez and Shaheen. To my love, Jaques de Silva, who has read and reread and will hopefully continue to read. And to my extended family who have been a constant source of inspiration.

For my friends: Leah, Neo, Simone, Mazuba, Hanneke, Naima, Ndoni and Mbali, who listened tirelessly. Caryn Peterson, your investment in this project goes above and beyond. Special thanks to Bontle Senne and Deborah Vieyra who helped get me to the finish line.

*Outside the Lines* was written as part of my MA in Creative Writing at the University of Witwatersrand. I would like to thank Professor Michael Titlestad and Bronwyn Law-Viljoen for guiding the process and my wonderful supervisor Craig Higginson for your insight. To Peter, Anna, Lawrence, Don and Adrian, it was a pleasure going on this journey with you.

My endless gratitude to Colleen Higgs and everyone at Modjaji Books for taking a chance on an unknown. And to my editor, Andie Miller, for getting the spinach out of my teeth.

# ABOUT THE AUTHOR

Ameera Patel is in the storytelling business and received recognition for this, being named one of the Mail & Guardian's Top 200 young South Africans in 2016. She is a Naledi award-winning actor as well as a writer, theatre-maker and facilitator residing in Johannesburg. She read for a BA in Theatre and Performance at the University of Cape Town in 2005 and in 2013 she received a distinction for her Masters in Creative Writing from Johannesburg's University of the Witwatersrand. As a writer Patel earned her stripes with Whistle Stop. It received a Silver Standard Bank Ovation Award (2014) and a PANSA New Writer's Award (2014). In 2018, Patel was commissioned to adapt Mary Watson's short-story *Jungfrau* into a play. The play premiered at The Theatreforemen Festival in Germany before returning to South Africa to perform at The National Arts Festival and at The ConCowan Theatre at UJ. Patel is currently working as a scriptwriter residing in Johannesburg. *Outside the Lines* is her debut novel.